THREE SHORT STORIES

of Faith, Hope and Love

Norma Clark

Three Short Stories of Faith, Hope and Love – Norma Clark

Published by Three in One Publishing 2024

The Passion Translation (TPT), New Testament with Psalms, Proverbs, and Song of Songs. Copyright 2018, Broad Street Publishing Group, LLC.
The Revised Standard Version of the Bible (RSV)

Printed by Pendlee Print 2024

Typeset in 12pt Calibri

Genre: Christian/Inspirational/Fiction

ISBN 978-1-3999-9139-1

Contents

Acknowledgements

Firstly, I have to thank my parents for (whatever their reasons) sending my two sisters and me to Sunday School every week at our local Anglican Church. There I learnt from a young age that Jesus was my friend.

Secondly, I would like to acknowledge Malcolm and John - two amazing friends that I entrusted a first reading of the stories to and who encouraged me not to put them back in the drawer but to take positive steps towards getting them published.

Thirdly, a special thank you to Elizabeth Webb who kindly and skilfully took me through the many hours of preparation and re-reading to bring it into the right format for publishing. Without her input it just wouldn't have happened.

And finally, of course, I acknowledge without any doubt, that my Heavenly Father gave me the stories and the words, and I was just the scribe who wrote them down.

Introduction

These short stories were written many years ago but, having brought them out and shared them with some friends, I have been encouraged to dust them off and get them printed.

We are living in a post-Christian age where God has become 'unnecessary' and mostly disregarded as we try to navigate life's challenges and inconsistencies. At a young age, myself and my two sisters (one older, one younger) were sent to Sunday School. I grew up knowing God as my friend. A regularly sung chorus still in my mind and often sung over my own crying children and grandchildren was *Jesus loves me, this I know, for the Bible tells me so.*
As I grew up, I might have drifted away and done some things I wasn't particularly proud of but always, in my need or life's choices, He was there and someone to turn to, and from whom I received wisdom and advice. A 'prop', some might say - but yes, what a prop! He wants to be involved in our individual lives and to be directing our paths - not in a dictatorial or controlling way - but in a loving and affirming way. He only desires the best for each one of us.

As a Christian, I know it is possible to have a personal relationship with a living God who knows me by name. He longs to show His love to each one of us. As one who has genuinely experienced healing, strength and wisdom in life and ministry through my faith, I wanted to find a way to share God's love and presence without being religious. I hope that these short stories, communicate in such a way that touch people of any age and bring them closer to the possibility of a relationship with God himself.

Norma Clark 2024

A Brief Summary of the Stories

Oh God, You Must Be Joking!

This is an allegory of the Bible story of the birth of Jesus found in the gospel of Luke. I was struck by either how familiar we may be with this historical account through many years of hearing it told, or completely unaware of it having had little or no Christian teaching. I have re-told it in the context of 'The Troubles' between the Republican and mainly Catholic Southern Irish and between the Protestant and British-connected Northern Irish. At the time of Jesus' birth Israel was an occupied country, and the people were often in conflict with the Roman governance who ruled over them and occupied their land. Not a direct correlation to the Irish situation of the 1970 – 1990s but enough to use the context for this story.

Tommy

This is entirely fictional but based on my experience of a tent 'crusade' in which a church (or a group of churches) reaches out into a new area, sometimes hiring a large marquee and putting on a series of meetings to which various speakers are invited along. These are usually well publicised, and invitations are sent all around the locality to encourage new people to come and hear the good news about God's love and plan for them and their lives.

Hot Coffee

This shorter story is also entirely fictional and recognises that, as much as we have a loving God who longs for a relationship with each of us, we also have a spiritual Enemy. His name is Satan and there is a real and on-going battle in the spiritual realm but because, after His crucifixion, Jesus was raised by God from the dead, He has - and always will have - the last word. He will win any conflict with Satan in any form. His victory means that there is power in the Name of Jesus to overcome every attack of the enemy. Anyway, I will let you read the story ...

Oh God, You Must Be Joking!

Chapter 1 - The Facts of Life

It was more than possible that had a pin been dropped at that particular moment, everyone would have known it. The giggles, whispers and knowing looks had subsided into a shocked silence.

'There now, I didn't mean to alarm you, just give you the facts and issue an adequate warning!' She collected her notes together and looked around the class, peering over her half-moon spectacles. Her tight grey curls and middle-aged plumpness belied the frankness and openness with which, under the non-descript heading of Health and Hygiene, she had brought the class face to face with the facts about Aids, venereal disease and other less harmful but equally undesirable 'communicable diseases,' as she had so graphically described them.

'I'm not judging anyone or telling you how to live your lives, but you have to realise that there will be consequences to any relationship you enter into, and you must be particularly aware of what you are doing when you choose sexual partners. I look forward to seeing you all next week.'

With these last words echoing and a great sense of achievement, she swept out of the classroom leaving the class in a temporary state of shock.

The stunned silence had erupted into a volcano of comment, indignation and awe. Saved from itself by the sound of the hooter, the class turned en masse towards the classroom door, spilling out into the corridor like a ribbon of toothpaste suddenly squeezed from its tube, merging into the stream of bodies already heading in the direction of lockers and cloakrooms. A tall slim girl hurried along with the rest, her infectious laughter and readiness to smile made her popular and noticed in the crowd. In a soft, but unmistakable Northern Irish accent, she addressed someone, somewhere nearby in the busy corridor.

'Come on Clare. Have you still got to collect your books? I'd like to catch the early bus tonight.'

'I'm just coming, what's all the hurry for anyway?'

'Greg is coming up this evening and I really need to get some study done first. I only get to see him once a week, so I want to make the most of the time we have together.' She tossed her dark hair out of her face and eyes twinkling, cast a knowing look across to Clare.

'Anne, you don't mean that you and Greg are going to ... not tonight after what we have just heard! What do you think about all of that - Aids and sexually transmitted diseases? Do you think it is really as bad as she made out just now? It couldn't happen to us, anyway, could it?'

Never usually at a loss for words, Anne hesitated, the milky white skin of her cheeks flushing a deep pink. 'Well actually,' she replied in a hushed voice, 'Greg and I haven't, that is, Greg really wants to wait until we are married.'

'Married,' exploded Clare, but you have been going out together for ages, and when will you get married? Greg has only just started his apprenticeship. It will be years yet - you can't wait all that time, Anne!'

'Well, that is what he has said. Anyway, you're not to tell anyone else, promise me Clare,' Clare smiled and nodded her head.

'Ok, ok, I promise,' she said quickly, knowing only too well that Anne's bag might come flying her way, more perhaps to cover her embarrassment than to cause Clare any real harm.

'Here's the bus, come on run for it.'

Half an hour later Anne alighted at her stop and waved goodbye to Clare. She walked thoughtfully up to the front door of her parents' comfortable four-bedroomed house. They lived on an estate, where the private houses had been delicately screened from the council houses on the other side of the road by a row of tall conifers. Anne's older sister, Marie, had already left home. She was away at college in England and Anne missed her company and uncomplicated friendship more than she liked to admit. Her parents had, of course, been glad to see one of their daughters move away from all the trouble and violence. The problems between North and South of the country constantly marked their lives, affecting every decision they had to make.

'Why we go on living in this God forsaken city, I don't know,' her mother would say in her clear Irish brogue every time someone was shot or blown up, an all too frequent occurrence these days. But this was their home, they all knew that Anne's father was a policeman a special branch officer and often working under cover. They lived in constant fear for his life these days.

***

Chapter 2 - The Dream

Anne turned the key and let herself in. The house was quiet and empty for once. The clean shining paintwork reminding her of the care and pride with which her mother viewed her role as homemaker. Anne wondered how she would cope with the long, lonely days when she, as well as her sister, had left the nest. The smell of lavender hung in every room. The shorter rays of the winter sun shining in through the glass panels of the front door couldn't find dust or finger marks to spoil the effect of the morning's efforts. Her mother, usually there to greet her, had to Anne's immense relief, gone to visit a friend for the afternoon. She was glad of some time for herself, especially to think before Greg came later on. The big question she needed time to consider was whether she should tell him about the dream or just try to put it out of her mind and forget all about it. She knew that Clare thought life was just for living as hard as you could, enjoying its privileges and pleasures but spurning its responsibilities. She knew she wasn't ready to confide in her yet.

'Who knows what tomorrow will bring?' Clare would often remind everyone within earshot. 'Have a good time while you can, that's my philosophy for life. Life is too short to take it too seriously.' Clare would probably dissolve into a fit of giggling and not understand her anxiety at all. Anne knew she couldn't cope with that kind of reaction just yet. They were good friends but so different. Anne, apparently outgoing and vivacious, thought a lot about the war going on around her. She grieved inwardly at the wanton destruction of her beautiful green land and wondered at the hatred deep in the hearts of men that they could feel justified in ripping it and the community apart - leaving scars and wounds that it seemed might never be healed. So many on both sides had suffered so much - what was the point of it anyway?

Anne made herself a pot of tea and took two of her favourite biscuits. She sat down in her father's big leather armchair in front of the fireplace. The grate had been laid ready for a fire later in the evening. She closed her eyes and relaxed, warmed by the hot tea, she began to doze. Deep rhythmical breathing indicated her lapse into a gentle sleep. Suddenly and without any warning her arm shot out sideways sending the precariously balanced cup and saucer flying. In the next instant she was awake, her heart thumping loudly and uncontrollably.

'No, no,' she whispered quietly and instantly to herself,

'It's just a dream, that's all, just a dream.' With great clarity she had witnessed again the exact situation she had had in a dream the night before. This is ridiculous her conscious mind protested. I'm not ready for that yet and anyway I've got my 'A' levels to do and then catering college, I really don't understand any of this at all.

She and Greg had tentatively and shyly approached the subject of how they felt about each other, and how far they should go to express those feelings. Greg had been adamant.

'I know it'll be hard - God knows, I love you, Anne. I have since the day I first met you, I've never wanted anyone else, but I want us to stay special to each other. I want our wedding night to be something special for both of us … our first night as husband and wife to be just that. Can you understand that Anne, can we wait for that?' She had squeezed his hand, nodding but not trusting herself to speak. She knew others who would laugh at such sentiment, but it had been to her a beautiful moment and a speech from Greg's heart which she treasured very much.

Now again, so vividly in her mind, she had seen herself and Greg on a train. Many others were travelling with them. Around her small children were becoming tired and irritable, wanting to know how much longer it was going to be and complaining that they were hungry or thirsty. Their luggage was piled around them, all the racks having been quickly filled. In the crowded train Greg stood beside her, his arm around her, her head resting on his hip. As the train had lurched, she had flung out her arm to keep Greg from falling on top of her. She could see now why she sat while others stood. Her usually trim figure was almost unrecognisable. She wore a large cotton smock over a pair of new denim jeans and was unmistakably many months pregnant.

The telephone shrilled. It's plaintive demanding call breaking the silence. She jumped, summarily dismissing the scene, but not its profound effect, from her mind. She lifted the receiver.
'Hello, yes hello, Greg, yes, I am alright - at least I think so. I - I will explain after tea, try not to be any later - I need so much to see you, I am so glad that you are on your way,' she added as she replaced the receiver back in its place.

Later that evening, they sat together in the small cosy sitting room. The fire crackled as it consumed its contents, sending orange and yellow flames leaping up the chimney, almost hypnotising Anne as she waited for Greg to say something. He was sitting in the armchair now and she was on the floor leaning back against his legs, his hand resting on her shoulder caressed her head and hair. It had been easier to talk to him with her back towards him. He had listened quietly, once or twice pausing in his stroking movements. They had the room to themselves for a while, Anne's mother having claimed she needed to be in the kitchen, to get some baking done. Anne's father was on the late shift which meant he probably wouldn't be home until the early hours of tomorrow, if it was a relatively good night.

Greg cleared his throat. 'Well, erm,' he began, uncertain how he was supposed to respond to such a delicate situation. 'It hasn't happened, has it Anne? I mean, of course you're not erm - pregnant, are you? And we agreed we would wait didn't we - so perhaps it is literally just a bad dream.' He laughed awkwardly at his own joke. Young though he was, he was able to step outside the emotion of the situation and look at it in its reality. She reached up to take hold of his hand.

'Yes,' she said, 'Yes, I'm sure you're right, it's probably everything getting on top of me, exams, things we have been discussing at school, the tension all around, thanks for not getting mad or laughing. I feel heaps better now I have told you.' A sense of profound relief flooded her whole being. She chattered on while Greg watched her, smiling and listening and just enjoying being with her again. '… and I did tell you about the dreadful Health and Hygiene talks we have been having at school. We have a very enthusiastic teacher called Miss Giddy, you daren't ask too …'

'Miss Giddy? You have got to be making that up.' Greg interrupted, 'No, no, I am most certainly not,' came Anne's reply. She attempted a look of disapproval such as Miss Giddy herself might have communicated by peering over the top of her spectacles. Greg snorted loudly and they dissolved into a helpless fit of giggling. As their laughter subsided, they looked at each other, smiling gently, appreciating each other. Greg leaned forward and kissed her forehead, then the tip of her nose and then on the lips. He held her head against his chest and told her how much he loved her.

***

Chapter 3 - The Message

'Do you need any help with the lunch today, Mum, only I thought I'd go down to the church this morning - if that is alright with you, or would you like to come as well?' Anne stated as nonchalantly as she could, the following Sunday morning. She hoped desperately her mother wouldn't start quizzing and probing to find out why she should suddenly want to go to church. Anne's mother, as mothers sometimes do, sensed the 'no questions' warning in Anne's delivery of her announcement, and she continued rolling out pastry for the Sunday apple pie.

'You carry on, darling,' she smiled, glancing at Anne over her shoulder, 'Your father should be off today and home at least by lunch time, I want to do him a really special dinner, and I am up to my elbows in flour. Everything alright at school is it, and between you and Greg?'
'Yes, yes, Mum, of course it is,' Anne replied, almost running across the kitchen and kissing her mother lightly on the cheek. She felt a great sense of relief not having to explain things she didn't understand too well herself. 'Thanks Mum, I will see you later.'

All part of growing up, her mother mused to herself. Sometimes she felt as if she was walking a tightrope. You had to be interested and ask questions, but not pry, to be sensitive when it was time for a heart to heart and to know when it definitely wasn't. You had to give compliments when that was wanted but not appear at any time to be condescending or overly enthusiastic at changes in fashion, hairstyle or wardrobe. She allowed herself a long deep sigh. She had noticed how thoughtful and serious Anne had become recently, and hoped that maybe this morning's excursion would help her to sort things out and perhaps find someone to talk to and confide in.

Anne slipped quietly into the back of the small Protestant church. People were already standing, singing a hymn. No one noticed her come in. She sat down and closed her eyes letting the sound wash over her. It was peaceful, anonymous, just what she had hoped. She allowed the service to roll on around her. Eventually, as yet more singing died away, a quietly spoken man in an ordinary grey suit stood to introduce a more grandly and brightly robed colleague.

'This is Monsignor Gardin, with whom I have the pleasure of an exchange of pulpits over the next couple of weeks. We are eager to demonstrate the possibility of friendship and co-operation between our two communities.' The two men nodded and smiled at each other.
'Monsignor Gardin has a very special kind of ministry, and I know that no one need go away from here this morning without a deeper knowledge of God.' He moved away from the microphone and gestured for the other man to come forward.

Anne's attention had begun to wander so that she wasn't really listening anymore, she wasn't quite sure now why she had felt that she should come down to the little church this morning. She had hoped to find some answer, some explanation for her dream, but really that was unlikely wasn't it, she mused to herself. It was the urgency, the intimacy of the man's deep gentle voice which caused Anne to drag her mind back from its meandering to pay attention to his next penetrating statement.

'There are people here this morning that God wants to minister to. He is here to heal the sick, to heal emotions, to meet every kind of need.' The speaker began to mention specific illnesses, specific situations. He was inviting people to come to the front of the church. One or two at first and then others moved forward to stand in front of him. Monsignor Gardin placed his hands on their heads and prayed for them out loud. Some stayed standing, some bowed their heads, whilst others fell gently backwards into the arms of a waiting helper who lowered them to the floor. Anne sat bolt upright now straining to see what was going on. Then Monsignor addressed them all again.

'These people have not fainted and have come to no harm, they have simply come under the power of God and He will be ministering to them in whatever way they may need. In a few minutes they will be able to return to their seats. If anyone still needs to feel God's love please do come forward, God's power is here this morning and there are others He is wanting to bless.'

Anne sat riveted to her seat. She longed to go forward and find out if this was for real. Did God really love her and want her to know it? Her legs wouldn't move, her heart was thumping so loudly and quickly it kept bumping and missing beats. She was quite sure the people nearby could hear it too. Why, oh, why couldn't she move? She closed her eyes …

'Oh God', she began under her breath … the clear authoritative voice rang out again.

'God is telling me, right now, that in this meeting His power is coming on a young lady and God is saying to you, 'Don't be afraid, be still.' Wherever you are sitting just let His power come upon you now. God has chosen you and He has a special purpose for your life. Don't be afraid … He will lead you and protect you. He is your God.'

Anne felt a warm glow begin at the top of her head, it moved down and across her whole body. Her heart stopped beating so fast, she relaxed, peace flooded her whole being. She sat quite still enjoying the warmth and radiance all around her. She knew God had been speaking those words directly to her. As everyone rose to sing the final hymn she slipped out as unobtrusively as she had come in. She didn't want to talk to anybody right now, only to be by herself. She needed time alone to think and to go on experiencing that deep feeling of love.

She walked down the tree lined path to the gate. At least here the grass grew undisturbed, and the birds still had branches to sing from and to nest in. The small garden surrounding the hall was like an oasis in the desert of destruction all around them. She stood still taking in the precious moments of tranquillity, listening to the silence, savouring the moment of peace within herself. She let herself out through the gate. Glancing back, she wondered how long the feeling would last. What had those words meant anyway? As she walked down the grey deserted road a thought so clear, and so unexpected, came into her mind. 'You are going to have a baby, Anne - He will be my son, The Son of God.' She heard herself gasp, a choking sort of gasp. Her legs suddenly felt like soft wet sponges that might fold beneath her at any moment.

'Oh no, oh God, you must be joking! Not that dream. You really can't have said what I thought you said.' She sat down on the wooden seat by the bus stop and dropped her head into her hands. Tears began to wet her cheeks and fingers. Was it really possible that a few moments ago she had felt an overwhelming sense of joy and happiness. Now she was gripped by a depth of fear and despair she had rarely known before.

'Why me, why is this happening to me? I don't want to be special or privileged, I'd much rather be just normal and ordinary.'

'Anne, I know it's not going to be easy for you, I never said it would be easy, that's why I had to choose someone I could trust, a fighter, a winner with a sense of humour. Your child, Anne, will be the Son of God. He is coming into this world to be its Saviour.'

'Oh dear, I must be dreaming again, this can't really be happening to me, can it? People only imagine things like this. I only hope that you are going to help me sort all this out at home and school and all that. What will everyone say? I can just hear the gossips now.

'Did you know?'

'Have you heard?'

'Not Anne, you can't be serious?'

'She had so much potential, she won't make it to college like her sister then?'

'Her poor mother, how must she feel, oh dear such a shame.'

Anne put her hands over her ears as if that would shut out the comments she could hear inside her head. 'Oh no,' she spoke quietly, almost despairingly to herself, as a new thought crashed through her mind.

'Dear God, what will Greg think? If I am really hearing all this from you, please speak to Greg, tell him what you are doing and help him understand. I don't want to lose him, I really don't. She shivered as she lifted her head from her hands. She didn't know how long she had been sitting on that hard, lonely seat. She knew it must be past one-o-clock, the time lunch on Sunday was always served promptly. Usually, they stood together whilst grace was being said, then the Sunday roast could be carved.

She was going to be late. She found a handkerchief, blew her nose and dabbed her eyes. She pulled a comb through her long dark hair and flicked her head back in the practised way she often used to toss the hair out of her face. She powdered her face hoping to hide the blotches. Half walking, half running, she arrived at the front door of her house. Even as she was removing the key from the lock her mother's voice rang out.

'Is that you Anne, are you alright love? We were beginning to get worried.' Anne popped her head round the dining room door. 'Sorry, Mum - Dad, I shan't be a second, glad you didn't wait for me ...' and she disappeared, mounting the stairs two at a time. Her parents exchanged glances.

'Not too many questions straight away, she will spill the beans in her own good time,' her father pronounced as he reached for the joint to carve Anne some meat.

'Yes, Dear, of course,' came the murmured reply, skilfully masking the surprise she felt at her husband's more gentle, sensitive approach to his daughter's uncharacteristic behaviour.

In front of her dressing table mirror, in her well used study-bedroom, Anne checked her appearance. Looking at herself and then around the room, she saw the scattered piles of textbooks and notebooks from which she had been studying. Tears filled her eyes again and the sight of her own reflection made her turn quickly away from the mirror. She took a couple of deep breaths, applied another layer of face powder and prayed that her parents wouldn't ply her with too many questions which she knew she wouldn't be able to answer right now.

'Help yourself to vegetables.' Her mother handed Anne her plate, the slices of meat carefully arranged on one side. 'Was it a long meeting or did they have coffee and time to meet and chat at the end?'

'No Mum, I had some things to think about, so I sat on a seat and completely lost track of the time. I didn't mean to worry you, I am sorry.' Anne was surprised by the simplicity and truth of her reply. 'I am going to explain everything to you both but perhaps I could do that when I feel ready and a bit more clear for myself.'

'Of course, dear, we are here to listen anytime we can be of help. That's all we want to do - be of help and understand what is bothering you just now.'

'Thanks Mum, I appreciate that.' Anne knew that was exactly what she was going to need. She could only hope that they both really meant it.

Later that afternoon as they cleared the dishes her mum, wanting some discussion and conversation with her usually tacit husband, offered, 'Don't you think she seems different, quieter, deeper, so young and yet it is as if she has suddenly grown up. She was in charge of that conversation at dinner you know, in control of herself and the whole situation. You don't suppose she is going to give up 'A' Levels do you, leave school or maybe thinking of going into the police force, not the pol ...'

'Mary, will you just listen to yourself going on so, give the girl a chance. She said she will tell us when she is ready. Now pass me that tea towel and let's get this finished. It's my afternoon off remember and I want to relax and enjoy it, so leave it now, eh?' He took the tea towel and gave her a quick kiss on the cheek in return. She smiled, a whole afternoon together, she hoped there wasn't anything good to watch on television then perhaps they could go out for a while, a walk or a short drive, so long as they were careful where they went. And he was right of course, Anne would tell them in her own good time.

***

Chapter 4 - Friendship

During the next couple of weeks life, it seemed to Anne, had returned to some semblance of normality. Her mind began to persuade her that, actually, her vivid imagination had been on overdrive. She became absorbed with the topics of conversation buzzing around the school. The current spate of sectarian murders, a death threat list which it was rumoured named top politicians and police officers, the massive bomb which had destroyed an army barracks in London, everyone discussing what action they considered the government should or could take to contain the escalating violence and anarchy. Most of the pupils in Anne's class were well into revising now, some looking tired and getting irritable as the strain and tension increased. With the exams just weeks away now and with unemployment rising, good results were vital. Travelling had become more hazardous with the constant threat of assault or kidnap. There was very little in the way of a social life for anyone living in the province these days - it was no longer safe to be out after dark.

Greg made his trips northwards most Saturdays. Sometimes he and Anne studied together or went for short walks. They often discussed what life would be like if there was peace. They had become so used to the war and the uncertainty of daily living. Perhaps they would eventually have to leave, although both knew their roots were deep in Ireland - North and South. Anne had told Greg about her visit to church, leaving out, for the time being, her own particular experience. Over the next week as she and Clare travelled to and from school together, Clare poured out the details of the rows she and Martin had been having with increasing frequency.

'On and off over the last month actually ...' she confessed, 'ever since that morning we began those Health and Hygiene lectures. What she said about love being much more than just the physical relationship, how really loving someone means caring, sharing, giving to each other, listening. It made me notice how things were when Martin and I were together. All he wanted was the kissing, petting and even so called 'making love.' I tried him out a couple of times saying - I had something important I needed to tell him, but he always said, 'Ok, Ok we can talk later, not now though.' Deep down I began to feel used, not loved and when I said that I didn't want so much of the physical side of things he seemed to get more irritable with me and rows seemed to flare up out of nowhere. Anne, I feel so lonely without him. There is a great big gap, and I don't know how to fill it. It wasn't a good relationship I can see that now, it couldn't have continued the way it was going, but I do miss seeing him.'

'Oh Clare,' Anne blurted, looking at her friend in a new light. 'I am so sorry, I have been so full of my own thoughts I hadn't noticed things weren't so good for you. I am sorry, but I'm not sorry you have split with Martin. This sounds a bit unlikely right now I know, but I am sure you will meet someone who will love you and care for you in the right way. In fact,' she added with a smile and a very knowing look, 'I have often seen David having a furtive glance your way, but everyone thought that you were Martin's girl and kept their distance ... '

'Anne, you don't think I will have caught anything do you? You don't suppose Martin had other, well, relationships. I couldn't bare it, just thinking about it makes me feel dirty.' She turned towards Anne, looking her straight in the eye, searching her friend's face to see if it registered shock or rejection. 'I do envy you now Anne, if only - oh those dreadful words. If only I had said no, I want to wait for a permanent relationship, I just didn't really think about it all enough. It seemed ok because everyone else talked about doing it as well.' Anne put her arm around her friend's shoulder, pleased they were talking now as close friends, sharing the things with each other they hadn't been able to tell anyone else about.

'I know I would be feeling the same as you are right now, but you mustn't forget how you felt about him. You were very fond of him, and you thought you loved him, didn't you? Don't be too hard on yourself, Clare. If you promise not to laugh, there is something I could share with you which might just help you to forgive Martin and yourself, clear away all the regrets and enable you to begin afresh.'
'Sure,' Clare responded warmly, glad of Anne's friendship, 'and I promise I won't laugh'. Why don't we stop off at my house for a cup of tea. We can phone your Mum and let her know where you are. To tell you the truth I would be glad of your company for a while.'

The two girls got off the bus, smiling a 'thank you' to the driver. They turned down the street towards Clare's house. They walked slowly thoughtfully, heads close together. Most of the way Clare said nothing, listening attentively as Anne recounted in some detail the events of her visit to the church. All except, of course, the part concerning herself and the baby. Clare didn't laugh. It seemed to her that maybe life needed to be taken more seriously than she had previously considered necessary. Perhaps it was time to start asking questions and finding answers.

'Do you seriously believe that a God exists, then Anne? Do you think that he can really care about each one of us? But we must be like loads of little ants all looking alike, rushing round being busy, trampling all over each other, building mounds, not really going anywhere. I mean is there really any point in minding how we live? You work hard at school to get a job, work hard at your job to get a better job, get married, work hard to get a better job to pay all the bills, spend twenty years bringing up a family who then go and leave you during which time you have to avoid fatal illnesses, car accidents, being blown up, shot or maimed. I just wonder if there is really any point to it all, Anne. A lot of hard work and heart ache for not very much in return - is all I can see ahead.

'I haven't got all the answers, Clare, I wish I had, but I do know that there is such a person as God, that He actually spoke to me and touched me the other week. I know that despite all the troubles around us, I have felt at peace. I know my life doesn't depend on chance anymore, it is being guided by God and I want to get to know Him better.'

They had arrived at Clare's house. They shivered as they let themselves in, the cold greyness outside seemed to invade the empty house.

'Are your parents always out when you get home,' Anne asked, realising how much she took for granted her mother's cheery voice which usually greeted her arrival or the mouthwatering smell of freshly baked bread or scones, her mother's speciality.

'You get used to it,' Clare replied as she swept round the room, putting on lights, lighting the fire and filling the kettle almost, it seemed to Anne, in one continuous movement.

'Tea or coffee?' she called through to Anne who stood near the fire waiting for the warmth to reach her from the spluttering flames.

'Tea, every time for me please,' came the reply.

'How long ago did you visit the church, and have you been back there yet? I've wondered about you recently, you have looked different more confident, more relaxed,

'Let's see,' Anne moved across the room to the picture calendar hanging in the centre of the wall. Except for the picturesque scene depicted there, the room was relatively plain and uncared for. The furniture was adequate but unexciting and little effort had been made to make the room welcoming or cosy. Even the umbrella plant in the corner hung it's leaves in a sad droopy kind of way. Anne shivered despite the fire. She concentrated her mind on the dates in front of her.

'Let's see,' she murmured again half to herself.

'About four, no, five weeks ago,' she turned to say it again more loudly so that Clare could hear her through the hatch between the kitchen and the sitting room.

'Five weeks ago,' she repeated and then her hand flew to her mouth, 'Oh, no, it can't be!' she gasped, the colour draining rapidly from her face.

Clare carrying the tray in saw Anne feel quickly for the chair to steady herself, she put the cups down quickly and moved across to her side.

'What is it, Anne, you look as if you have seen a ghost, what's the matter, are you ill - shall I call a doctor?'

'No, no, I'll be alright in just a moment. Clare, could you call my Mum and let her know that I am here. I should have done that as soon as we arrived. I'll just sit here for a few moments, I will soon feel better, thanks ever so ...'

Clare put her arm around her friend's shoulder and gave her a squeeze.

'Of course, I will, then you are going to tell me what this is all about.' As Clare left the room to make the call, Anne covered her face with her hands.

'This is it,' she said aloud, 'If this is for real there are going to be a lot of consequences to face and difficult situations to handle. You said, 'Don't be afraid,' but I am afraid, and you will have to help me every step of the way.' As she paused to take a deep breath, Clare came back into the room.

'That's settled then, your Mum said to give her a ring when you are ready to go home and she will come and pick you up. Did I hear you talking to someone just then?'

'Only myself and ... God,' Anne lifted her head. A faint smile crossed her face as she turned towards Clare.

'There was more to my story about going to church. A few days before that I had had a very strange dream.' Anne poured out the whole story glad of a chance to tell someone properly at last.

'It all sounds so impossible, so ridiculous,' she finished, 'but when I looked at the calendar just now, I realised that my period is a week overdue. Clare, it is never normally late … Oh Clare what am I going to do?'

Clare refilled Anne's half empty cup of tea and slipped a sugar lump into it, she stirred it vigorously and handed it to Anne.

'First, drink this, you need it. Then let's go back and look at the whole situation very calmly. A week late isn't very much, nobody does anything until they have missed at least for a few more weeks. It may just be exam nerves and tensions. You haven't been on a diet, have you?' she added with a note of hope entering her voice, as she gave Anne a quick look over. 'That always upsets periods. It can cause them to stop altogether if you lose weight too quickly.'

'No, no Clare, I just wasn't ready to believe it. I was enjoying my new self and what God had done for me, but I wasn't ready to become the mother of His Son. I wasn't willing to look a fool, to look like I had got pregnant when I was still at school. I didn't want to give up any future career or bring shame on my family - but that was just seeing the situation from my point of view. God has seen the mess we are in, and he just wants to help us out of it. If He has really chosen me to do this, then I am honoured, and I will go through with it even if no one believes me. Clare you will stick with me, won't you? You won't disown me or giggle with the others behind my back, will you?'

Clare was quiet for a few moments before responding, 'I'm not sure I understand all this, but I do want to, it all feels more important than anything else right now. I want you to tell me all you know about God, and I promise I will be right with you whatever is going to happen. I have got more time now, now that Martin and I have … split. We can study together and find out about pregnancy, and God, and all that. You will still be able to take your exams. You might be getting a little bit fatter by then, but nobody will notice. We can say that you have been snacking too much whilst studying and you have put on a bit of weight.' She paused and laughed a little nervously, wondering what Anne was thinking, 'If it does all turn out to be true that is ...'

The two girls turned towards each other, Clare held out her arms and they hugged and held each other close for the next minute. When they drew away from each other, tears had fallen wetting both their faces and revealing the new emotions and closeness of friendship they had both discovered. They fumbled in their pockets for handkerchiefs.

'Whew, this is deep stuff,' Clare confessed as she dried her eyes, wiping them carefully so as not to smudge her mascara too much.

'I will wait another month before I tell my parents, there is no point in putting them through the 'ifs' and 'buts' until it's all confirmed and they have to face it for what it is,' Anne mused half to herself and half out loud to Clare.

Recovering now from the initial shock, she felt just the suspicion of excitement mixed with apprehension beginning to rise up on the inside of her.

'I will call Mum now to come and pick me up, it will be another fifteen minutes before she gets here, time to regain our composure and plan our strategy,' she winked at her friend and smiled properly now. 'Thanks for everything, Clare,' she added with emphasis and warmth.

***

Chapter 5 - The Revealing

Several weeks later, on a bright but snowy Sunday afternoon, Greg, Anne, and Anne's father sat stiffly and awkwardly round the dining room table. Eventually to everyone's relief her mother appeared at the dining room door with a cheery, 'Well, here we are then.' She had carefully set a tray of teacups and a large pot of tea down on the table. 'Surely nothing can be as bad as all that,' she smiled as she looked at each one in turn. Dinner had already been an unusually tense occasion. It wasn't often that Greg was able to join them for a formal meal and everyone had been on their best behaviour. Anne had already indicated that she and Greg had something they wanted to talk over with them. Of course, her parents had speculated over the last few weeks, now this request and Greg's presence seemed to confirm their growing, nagging fears that the two wanted to get engaged and possibly leave school without ever making it to college.

'It's bound to be a strain on them, only being able to see each other once a week,' her mother had said with a deep sigh of understanding, as she had tentatively raised the subject with Harry the previous evening.

'So it was for us and plenty of others like us,' her husband had replied. 'I am sorry, Mary, seventeen is just too young to know your own mind on such important issues. They can wait another couple of years yet. Anyway jumping the gun a bit aren't we, we don't know what they want to talk to us about yet,' and he noisily folded his paper and slid, it seemed to Mary, an inch lower in his favourite armchair, down behind the pages.

'Shall I pour?' she enquired of everyone in general, trying her best to lighten the atmosphere, and keep the occasion relatively relaxed. She handed out cups of steaming hot tea.

'Thanks. The best china,' Anne murmured appreciatively, responding to her mother's efforts with a reassuring smile as she took her cup. 'If we are all sitting comfortably - then I'll begin.' She laughed slightly nervously but determined not to be intimidated by her father's serious and anxious expression.

'This is, of course serious, I know, but it really needs talking about with sensible discussion and no hysteria. It's not easy to talk about or handle and I am really going to need the help you offered me a few weeks back, do you remember that Mum, Dad? That morning when I came back from church very late and I promised I would explain when I was ready, you said your main concern was to help me if I needed it. I really appreciated the trust and space you gave me then and I am sure as I explain you will understand why that was important and why I am going to need to take up that offer of help over the next few months.' Her lip quivered, she was determined not to cry but so many emotions seemed to be welling up inside her all at once. She didn't know which would be harder to bear, their kindness and understanding, or their anger and disappointment. She knew there would have to be an initial reaction from them, and she expected that it would be a pretty strong one at that.

At that moment as they were waiting, each with their own thoughts, Anne's mind took her back to that last evening with Greg. He had held her hand and gone unbearably quiet when eventually she had told him everything, that it was true, that it was all actually happening, she was expecting a baby. That the girl he had wanted to marry, the perfect bride, was going to be an unmarried mum!

Poor Greg, she had felt very sorry for him, how could any man cope with such a shattering of his hopes and dreams. She knew it would break her heart if he left her, but how could she expect him to stay? The silence had seemed interminable to Anne, anything else would have been easier to handle - anger, reproach, questions, anything rather than just the silence.

'I will hate it Greg if you decide to finish it between us, but I will understand. I know it must be awful for you. There really isn't any easy way to tell someone that you are pregnant when you are not married, is there?' He had turned and looked straight at her then, his eyes taking in every detail of the face he thought he knew so well. He had seen the openness and anguish, the honesty and hope, he only knew he loved her so much.

'I don't know what to say. Yes, I am disappointed, of course I am, but then sometimes our dreams are too near to perfection to reach anyway, aren't they? I think I could get used to the idea of being a dad, in fact I spent quite a few journeys thinking about the possibility after you had told me about the dream.' He paused, not sure how to say what he knew had to be said. They had always promised each other to tell everything, no hidden resentments, no niggles left to fester, just openness and honesty with each other. Now he had to put that resolve to the test.

'You must understand Anne that I am not exactly questioning you, but I must express exactly what I am feeling right now and it's hard. Do you hear what I am saying Anne?' Anne nodded, not really trusting herself to speak, knowing what he must say, she saw the consequences as being inevitable.

'The real problem is grasping what you are saying about it being God's. I mean no one is going to believe that, are they? I am not sure I can, but then I get the worst nightmare of all thinking about how on earth you got pregnant. I know you are not a liar, Anne, but how can I believe what you have told me. How could God do such a thing and why us? No one, and I mean no one, is ever going to believe this, they will reckon we are just cranks or trying to make excuses for our own behaviour, and some of them are going to have to know.'

He paused, twisting in his chair to look from the floor to the window, making quite sure he didn't catch Anne's eye on the way. He knew he was adding to her anguish, thrusting and plunging a knife into an already raw, open wound. He knew that if he looked at her now, his heart would break, and he would leap across the room and just take her in his arms. He had had to voice his doubts, his fears, otherwise they would always be hanging there between them, spoiling things in the future. Had he and Anne got a future together? Could he walk out of that room now and leave her? Did he love her or just want to help her out of this mess she had got herself into?

Something like a great raw pain shot through his chest, he could no more walk out of that room and leave her behind than jump off a high building. He smiled a small rueful smile to himself, it had taken this crisis to realise how much Anne meant to him. He had begun to take her for granted, assuming she was there for him, that one day, when he was ready, he would have asked her to marry him. Now the situation had been snatched from his grasp, but it was still his to take and mould if he wanted to. And, oh, how he wanted to have Anne and the baby, Anne's baby. He shivered slightly with a growing sense of excitement and responsibility. With his back still slightly towards Anne he spoke again, slowly, deliberately.

'Our parents are the first people we must speak to and if we get their understanding ...'

'We,' she heard herself whisper, 'Did you say, 'we' Greg, do you mean that you are willing to go through this with me? I was afraid even to hope, to think of the possibility of us ... together.'

'Together and married', he had responded in a resolute but gentle tone of voice, 'we will get married in the summer holidays ...' His suggestions for tackling the situation were brought to an abrupt end as Anne's feelings of relief and gratitude broke from her in deep, shuddering sobs. The volcano of emotions she had pushed down for so many days and weeks had erupted from deep within her. He had taken her in his arms, holding her firmly and securely, kissing the top of her head and running his hand through her hair until her sobs calmed and she sat quietly leaning into him. 'I can only think this is going to be one awesome baby,' he murmured.

Now, today, he was here beside her giving her his support as she explained it all to her father and mother ...

'Yes, dear, your father and I had been wondering.' Mary's voice trailed away as Greg cleared his throat and looked at Anne in a way as to offer to take over the explanation for her. She squeezed his hand and nodded, too choaked and concerned for her parents' reaction and reputation to trust herself to speak again for the moment.

'Anne has been asked to fulfil a very special role in life, I always knew she was unique, now someone else has recognised her worth too and requires her help.' Sitting next to her he had smiled at her with pride and put his arm around her shoulder.

'Oh,' Anne's father sort of grunted, 'no one has said anything to me about it - what sort of thing?'

'That's why it is so hard to explain,' Anne continued, 'because we know you might think we are making the whole story up. I can only emphasise that everything we are telling you is the absolute truth. That Sunday when I went to church, I went because I had had a dream which had troubled me greatly. It had been so real, as if it was actually happening and I wanted to understand what it meant.' She continued uninterrupted until the whole story was told. She knew an incredible sense of relief once she had actually said that she was pregnant and expecting a baby.

'But it isn't Greg's or anyone else's, I absolutely swear that to you both.' She picked up her cup of cold tea, glad to have something to concentrate on.

Her mother was quiet, pale and speechless for once. She had opened her mouth to interrupt on several occasions, but no sound had resulted. Her father, by complete contrast, had gone an alarming shade of red. Anne wasn't sure whether he was in a furious rage or deeply embarrassed.

He rose from his chair pushing it back noisily, hands behind his back in a kingly fashion, he began to pace the length of the room.

'Well, this is a turn up for the books, isn't it?' he retorted as he turned on his heels for the third time. He was an uncomplicated sort of man, usually secure in life's familiar patterns. These days everything was becoming less and less predictable, in other people's lives out there in the streets - now it was happening here in his house, in his safe peaceful castle had come turmoil, a major upset that wasn't just going to go away like a bad dream. How he wished that he was just in the middle of his usual Sunday afternoon nap, instead of having to handle this most difficult situation.

'You are quite sure are you, Anne? Tests can be misleading and unreliable you know,' he turned again.

'I haven't been for any tests, Dad, but I am sure about this - there isn't any doubt. I will be able to finish this term off at school and sit my exams with everybody else, no one need know, especially if I am wearing summer dresses. Then I will go away, if that will make it easier for you and Mum, to Greg's farm perhaps or to Aunt Dolly's. She asks when I am going to see her every time she is on the phone. I don't want you and Mummy disgraced or ashamed, nor do I want to give the gossips something to talk about.'

'That is easier said than done, I'm afraid, my girl. I don't mind admitting this has come as quite a shock. I think you should go and put the kettle on for another cup of tea, your mother looks as if she might need one'.

'I am so sorry to give you more to worry about, I know life is already difficult for you both,' she tried to offer a weak sort of smile towards her mother as she made towards the door and ran her hand across her mother's quiet, hunched shoulders in an effort to comfort her.

Greg had sat quietly, determinedly, waiting for his moment, waiting until the first moments of shock had passed and, mentally at least, everyone was moving onto the next stage. He cleared his throat, wanting to speak loudly and clearly enough to catch everyone's attention, but not in any way wanting to be overloud or too harsh in his anxiety.

'With your permission sir, I would like to marry Anne as soon as the term finishes.'

For the first time since she had heard the news Mary lifted her eyes from the table, where they had remained glazed and wet staring at the mark she had missed with her duster. She wondered how on earth she had missed it, she was always so thorough, so careful with the cleaning. She raised her head looking up at Greg. He stood by the french doors, tall and slim, his body half turned towards the garden, but poised too, to move back into the room and into the centre of this family's life at a moment's notice.

'That's extremely thoughtful of you Greg, but we wouldn't dream of putting you in such a sacrificial position, would we dear?' Mary replied quietly, her voice and composure having returned at last. 'This is our problem, and Anne's, and somehow we will sort it out together.'
'No, no, you don't understand, it's not like that, really it's not,' he interjected quickly. 'I haven't asked Anne to marry me out of any sense of pity or necessity, I want to marry her because I love her. I, and not anyone else, will take care of her and - the baby,' he added more gently, 'besides I know she is telling the truth. After she had told me what had happened, I too tried a prayer, I asked God to show me as well as Anne what was happening here. In broad daylight I saw the clearest scene before my eyes. I have never experienced anything like it before, like a vision. I saw myself carrying a baby, Anne walking beside me, we were looking at empty flats. Looking, I presume, for somewhere to live. It wasn't around here, I am not sure exactly where we were, but I was carrying a baby.'

'Marry Anne in the summer, you say, eh, yes, maybe that would be for the best. Of course, she won't be able to start college in September, but perhaps a year later, we can make some arrangements for the baby then. She would have married you sooner or later, eh, lad, so things aren't so bad, could be worse I suppose. Thanks Greg, I know you will take good care of her.'

Harry turned towards his future son in law offering his hand in friendship. The two men shook hands and then gripped each other in a brief but genuine embrace. For the first time for hours Harry smiled and relaxed, at last they knew the worst and it really wasn't so bad once you knew. In fact, he was already beginning to contemplate the esteemed title of grandfather.

Anne had returned with fresh tea, seeing the two men talking and embracing, her father actually smiling she had deposited the tea tray as quickly as she was able and moved across to her father's side. Hugging him, letting him hold her close for a moment or two she simply told him that she loved him - and Mummy she added, leaving her father and walking round to her mother, still sitting quietly at the table. She put her arms around her neck and gave her a kiss and a squeeze too.
'I love you too Mummy. I love you both so much.'

'I think I will go and have a rest now, I am tired, so very tired.' her father confessed, 'I will leave you three to do the real talking and planning. Now, wake me at four, will you dear?' He looked across at his wife with a fleeting smile of reassurance.

***

Chapter 6 - The Plan

The month of June and the dreaded exams arrived simultaneously, much too quickly it seemed to most of the pupils in Anne's form. Anne, now over the first nauseating weeks of pregnancy felt strangely optimistic and flowing with health. She wished she could see the same zest for life in Clare. Clare had not felt well for some time, and the two girls had jokingly reckoned that Clare was suffering in sympathy with Anne. Unlike Anne though, Clare had not picked up and recovered her strength but felt tired and sick quite a lot of the time.

'A good holiday - that's what she needs. It was a long hard winter for everyone. Why don't you invite her to spend a few weeks with you at Aunt Dolly's?' her mother had suggested when Anne had told her about her concern for Clare.

'After all this time, two young ladies to visit me. What a treat,' her aunt had exclaimed when the request was made. 'They will be company for each other and will save Anne getting bored with me all the time.' She had taken the news of Anne's pregnancy better than anyone had expected, in a very matter of fact way, almost as if she wasn't surprised at all!

'We will have a good chat about it all when you get here,' was all the comment she would make, 'and you are more than welcome whatever has happened.' It was all agreed. When the exams were finished, they were free to leave school. Clare and Anne planned, packed, and booked their train.

Life in the country was altogether different to the routine both girls knew in the city. It was quiet, peaceful and very beautiful. Here they could relax, suddenly aware of how tight they had become over the last few months. There were no craters in the road, no vast piles of rubble where a house had once stood, no fear, only freedom. Freedom to walk along roads and footpaths, across fields of ripening wheat and corn, to travel by bus into the local town where they could shop or browse to their hearts' content. They sat in the garden, eating their lunch, reading or dozing. Clare, it seemed to Anne, ate less and less and dozed more and more. Far from looking healthier and rested as the days passed, she was losing weight and had become quieter and more withdrawn. Anne worried about her friend and even Aunt Dolly began to fuss more over Clare than over Anne. While Anne bloomed and grew gently larger, Clare became thinner and more and more lethargic.

'I don't really want to go, it has been wonderful staying here, but I must take Clare home,' Anne explained to her aunt. 'Clare won't admit it, but she isn't well. We can both see that, she must go and find out what is wrong. She keeps telling herself it is nothing, but she hasn't made any improvement in spite of the rest and sooo good food you have so wonderfully supplied us with. I am refreshed and ready to face the future. I will probably go and stay with Greg's family for a couple of weeks and learn a bit about farming along the way. I might need a crash course if I end up being a farmer's wife sooner than I thought!'

On their return home Clare's doctor immediately referred her to a specialist at the general hospital.

'What on earth can it be?' Anne's mother mused as the two of them sat in the kitchen, drinking their afternoon cup of tea and catching up on each other's news from the last six weeks. Cakes cooking in the oven filled the air with a delicious aroma. Mary realised how lonely she had been and how much she had missed Anne's cheery presence around the place. She watched her now with pride, her slim figure was filling out nicely now, her complexion was clear and delicately coloured by the fresh air and sunshine.

'You look so well, Anne, and happy. No regrets, not going to college this year with your friends? I wish you weren't going away again quite so soon, I do miss your company. Your father is working to breaking point. He is either out, asleep, or very poor company. I know it isn't his fault, but sometimes I feel as if I am living with a stranger, and he is irritable all the time.' Anne reached out and covered her mother's hand with her own.

'I am so sorry Mummy, just when things should be easier for you and Daddy should be looking forward to retirement - life is more fraught and unpredictable than ever. Do you think the British will bring the troops into Ireland and just occupy the whole country. If the terrorists are ever to be completely removed it may be the only way?'

'I pray God that we might have peace soon, one way or another, I don't think we have much left to keep resisting with. Our nerves are shattered, our hospitals full or blown up, our shops empty or threatened and the whole country is weary and exhausted.'

'I won't be away so long this time,' said Anne, 'I must travel while it is still comfortable to do so, and it will be nice to see Greg for a bit longer than the odd day or weekend. I have missed him so much. Then I will be home again until after the baby is born and Greg and I decide where we are going to live,' She stood up and bent to kiss her mother on the cheek.

'Of course, dear, I know you and Greg have got to make your own life now and I have got to make the best of mine for the time being. Oh! the cakes, I nearly forgot them. Pass me the oven gloves would you, darling.'

They had postponed the actual wedding until the end of the summer when Greg would be free to have some time off. He was a vital part of the work force over the summer months and until the harvest was finished. Anne thoroughly enjoyed being with him, seeing him at work, having his company at mealtimes and in the evenings. She would take cool drinks and sandwiches out to the men working the harvesters and sit eating with them, gradually getting to know more intimately other members of Greg's family. In the evenings, they took gentle walks through fields and down many quiet country lanes across and around the farm. Anne couldn't ever remember such a feeling of contentment. She could live here, she mused, in this beautiful valley. One day this farm would be Greg's, theirs, a place where children could grow up in peace and in safety, a place where children could be children, not forced by circumstances to grow up too quickly.

Greg's family were reserved and not very communicative when Anne first arrived. They made very little conversation and carried on as if there was nothing very unusual about Anne's appearance. Unusually quiet and slow to express their feelings Anne thought she would burst if someone didn't say something to her soon about the baby, even if it came out as an angry tirade it would at least have cleared the air and allowed her to tell her version of events.

'Be patient, darling, they are taking their time getting to know you, they won't talk about such a delicate issue with someone they still feel they don't know very well. You'll see when you have relaxed here, that when you are least expecting her to, Mother will just raise it all very matter of factly and before you know it, you and she will be the best of friends and sharing everything.'

'Oh, I do hope so,' Anne replied as they sat together before supper one evening. 'She has been so good to me in every other way, and I am loving being with her and with you Greg, it's, it's all so normal and beautiful.'

Several days later, Anne was sat in the old farmhouse kitchen scraping potatoes ready for the evening meal. The late afternoon sun, warm and full of summer glory, streamed in through the open door. It's long golden rays revealing the streaks of colour in Anne's usually black head of hair. She looked radiant, content and very beautiful as she sat willingly helping with all the ordinary jobs that had to be done around the place. As she watched her future daughter-in-law, Nancy felt her heart swell and lift with unexpected emotions of pride and love. She brushed a tear from the corner of her eye. They hadn't known quite how to react when Greg had first told them the news. They, of course, hadn't expected him to think of marriage yet and especially and under these circumstances. They had been so afraid that he was rushing into something he might regret later. One day the farm would be his if he wanted it, he would need a wife who knew farming and could work alongside him. They had met Anne who seemed such a city girl and hardly suitable as a farmer's wife, but suddenly, right here and now, Nancy knew it was going to be alright. She moved swiftly across the room and offered Anne a big smile putting her arm around her shoulders, 'You are welcome here anytime, my love, and I think you and Greg will be very happy together … and, of course, the baby too. Anne stood up quickly, 'Oh, Nancy, thank you so much' as she returned the hug with great warmth. 'I have been so afraid of what your reaction might be, especially to me being pregnant.'
'Well,' she said, 'Greg did try to explain. I am not sure I completely understood but what is done, is done … and we can't not welcome a new little farmhand, can we?'

Later that evening, Anne was sitting with Greg on a wooden seat outside the house watching the sun descend towards the horizon when Mr O'Rourke came running out from the house.

'A telegram for you, Anne. The boy wants to know whether you will be sending a reply.' Anne opened it carefully, reading the contents out loud.

'Return home immediately, no delay, explain on arrival.'

'Whatever can have happened, Anne? I'll come with you. Father can manage here without me now. The reply is, 'Will arrive tomorrow,' Greg announced, taking immediate charge of the situation.

***

Chapter 7 - Kindness and Visitors

They arrived home to be greeted with the news that all dependents of high-ranking police and army personnel were to be evacuated immediately. A new series of threats against the civilian population had been issued and already the casualties were mounting up. Pregnant, and with a southern Irish fiancé, Anne was deemed to be especially vulnerable. She had to be ready to leave on a train and ferry which had been specially provided by the government. It would be leaving the main line station the following morning. They shopped and packed as well as they could and the following morning, after many hugs and promises to keep in touch, Harry took them to the station.

They boarded the already crowded train, their hastily assembled luggage around them. Greg stood beside Anne who was occupying one of the last available seats.

'Do you know Greg, I am not sure whether to laugh or cry. It was such a rush getting back home, saying goodbye to everyone and trying to think of everything we might need, and me being so limited just now at doing things and moving about quickly. I am not afraid, though, I know that things will work out somehow. Do you remember my dream, the one that upset me so much at the time - this is exactly the scene I saw all those months ago of us both on a crowded train with me sitting because I was so obviously pregnant, and you stood beside me with other people and luggage all around us.' She looked up at Greg with a smile and squeezed his hand. It was now her re-assuring him that things would turn out well in the end.

The plan was that they should travel to the mainland by ferry and then on to Liverpool by train where temporary accommodation was to be made available to them. On their arrival they were to report to the main social security office who would redirect each traveller to suitable empty council flats or to Bed and Breakfast accommodation. The ferry crossing had been rough, and the boat had been crowded too. Of course, they had cat-napped, but not been able to sleep at all properly. They were tired, hungry and in a totally new environment. In spite of all their conviction and courage they now felt lonely and a bit lost.

They had been the last ones off the train from Holyhead. Anne had waited until the crowd had dispersed a bit, she had also begun to have spasms of pain across her back and couldn't move very quickly. When they eventually arrived at the office a dishevelled, but official, young man was just about to close the window and lock up the office. He looked the two weary young people over, quickly assessing their predicament.

'I am so sorry, I have just given out the last on my list of accommodation, there are no more rooms available tonight, I'm afraid.' Anne groaned as another spasm shot across her back. She leaned on Greg.

'We have to find something,' Greg looked at the young man with some desperation in his eyes and voice. 'Are you ok, Anne?' He turned back to the official, slight panic now rising in his voice, 'The pains seem to be starting to come more regularly and she is very tired, this could be early contractions. The last two days have been quite traumatic, the journey was long and crowded. Anything will suit us, you must know of somewhere or someone who could help us, please!'

'We ... ll, it's not a thing I would usually do but I can't leave you like this. Sit the lady down here and I will bring the old banger round. My Mrs'll make up the spare bed, if you don't mind a night in the armchair,' he glanced up at Greg, 'she'll love fussing round looking after the young lady'.

'Oh wow!' Greg exclaimed, "Thanks, thanks, a lot.' Greg was both surprised and extremely grateful.

The young couple settled Greg and Anne as comfortably as possible and as Anne's contractions increased, they prepared for her to be in labour. By five the following morning Anne had been delivered of a beautiful baby boy. It had been decided not to move her to hospital since she and the baby were both comfortable and doing well. Their amazing hosts had insisted they stayed right where they were until Anne was ready to move and a place had been found for them to go to.

'Top of my list you are this morning,' Matt, the young officer, said. 'No sweat, I will find you somewhere soon. Just take it easy and rest now, both of you.'

Their absolute kindness just caused Anne to keep bursting into tears, already very emotional over the safe and easy arrival of her son, she was overwhelmed by their spontaneous friendship and generosity. What little they had for themselves they insisted on sharing with her and Greg.

Anne was dozing later that afternoon, the baby asleep beside her. Their rest suddenly broken by a loud and insistent knocking at the front door.

'Hope we are not intruding Mr. We were sitting round having a bite of lunch when this bloke appeared out of nowhere, or so it seemed. Couldn't understand it really. Anyway, he said to call at this number in this road and we would see a special – baby, like?' Greg opened the door wider and stood aside to let them pass. Three well-built labourers walked into the small hallway. A younger lad, following behind them, suggested they removed their mud-clogged boots before going any further.

'The baby is upstairs sleeping. Please just wait here whilst I let my wife know she has visitors.' Anne came downstairs and, once she was sat comfortably with the baby on her lap, four men came in two at a time, quietly and respectfully. They looked in amazement sensing something extraordinary here but not quite knowing what it was. When they left sometime later, the oldest of the men pressed an envelope into Greg's hand. Just something we all put together to see you through the next few weeks,' he said, smiling and nodding with absolutely no intention of it not being accepted.

During the next few days, a steady stream of very different kinds of people called, each with a slightly different story, but all asking if they might see a baby, whom they believed to be at this particular house and to be someone special. Some arrived with gifts, groceries, baby 'things,' clothes, money and most spectacular of all, a nearly new 'Mini.'

'I don't think I will ever be lonely again,' Janine exclaimed as she rushed around making cups of tea, helping Anne with the baby and keeping her flat in some semblance of order in the circumstances. 'Nothing like this has ever happened to me before, I am going to find life terribly dull when you have gone. May I come and visit you when you are all settled in?'
'Absolutely, Janine. You had better, or I will want to know why not!' Anne responded immediately. The warmth of the newfound friendship between these two young women was unmistakable.

A few weeks later, true to his promise, Matt had found them a flat and they were able to settle into their own place just a few blocks away from him and Janine. Anne found herself both excited and apprehensive.

'What happens to us now, where do we go from here, do you think we can return to Ireland soon? What is this adorable little bundle going to mean for us?'
'Questions, questions but no answers.' Greg ruffled her hair affectionately.

'Hey, look a taxi has just stopped right outside. Who knows our address yet? It's just the taxi man coming to the door, I will see what he wants.'

'Mr O'Rourke, is it? There's a young girl in my car asking for you and a baby. Looks quite poorly to me, wouldn't let me take her to the hospital, insisted I brought her here.'

'I will be out right away. Another visitor, I think darling, back in a second.' Greg called to Anne as he followed the man out to the waiting taxi.

'Clare, good heavens, how did you get here?' He tried hard to hide his surprise at the way she looked as he helped her, putting her arm around his shoulder and supporting her up the steps into their home. Anne, shocked by her friend's appearance, settled her in their one armchair. As they embraced, they both started to speak together.

'There is some money for the taxi in …'

'How did you know where to find us? … It's alright Greg is paying the taxi man …'

'Where is he … the baby, Anne? I know He can help me. You said He was coming as the Saviour, because this world is in such a mess. Anne I am in a dreadful mess, please can I see Him, touch Him?' Anne stooped over the oval laundry basket sitting innocently in the corner of the room. Gently and lovingly, she lifted a bundle out and with the infant in her arms she crossed the room to Clare.

'Here he is, come on my darling, come and see 'Aunty Clare'. Her arms too weak to take him and hold him. Anne laid the baby in Clare's lap. She wiggled her fingers into his hand until He curled them around gripping tightly. He gurgled contentedly. As Anne stood watching, she saw a beautiful smile cross Clare's face and the colour coming back to her cheeks as she stretched out her arms, then her legs. Anne could see her friend's strength returning, the look of weariness and death had left her face. She turned towards Anne, radiant …

Clare stayed with them for a while all the time getting stronger and helping with jobs around the flat. One morning as she was making preparations to return home, she turned to Anne and said, 'Do you know Anne, I am feeling completely well again, and it all began the moment I arrived and held your beautiful little boy. So, whatever has happened here, God definitely wasn't joking. He is one special baby!'

'I have no idea what the future might hold but I am ready for the journey. Oh, God,' Anne whispered reverently, 'This was no joke!'

***

Oh God! You Must Be Joking! – Epilogue

This story is, of course, based on the well-known account of Jesus' birth found in the Bible in Luke's Gospel, Chapter 1:26-38. I have tried to bring the events into a time, and with circumstances that more nearly portray what this momentous event may have looked like in a more recent era.

What does *not* change is the difference that meeting and knowing Jesus, at any stage in our lives, can make. We have known many examples of healing and restoration of lives through such an encounter.

***

Tommy

Chapter 1

Tommy ran breathlessly down the road. His heart was beating faster than he had ever felt it before. He burst through the front door. 'Mum, Mum', he shouted, 'look what is going to be on tomorrow, look, Mum, look.'

His mother came down the stairs, tying the cord of her faded red dressing gown tightly round her tiny waist. Dark rings under her eyes revealed the tiredness and weariness she felt constantly these days. Sleep allowed her only a temporary escape from the pain in her body. She worried a great deal about the situation she and Tommy were in. Annoyed now with Tommy - she had told him so many times to come in quietly so that he didn't disturb her.

'What is it?' she asked tersely, 'It had better be important for all that row and waking me up!'
'Sorry Mum,' he muttered. All the excitement he had felt moments earlier seemed to drain out of the ends of his worn scuffed shoes. He watched her coming slowly down the stairs. He could see how thin she was getting, her hip bones showing their shape clearly under the soft folds of her dressing gown. Her face so different now from the one which smiled out to him from the photograph in her bedroom, no longer smiling and full of life but thin and lined and with a strange eerie colour. He pulled a crumpled piece of paper out

of his jacket pocket, with one hand behind his back, his two fingers tightly crossed, he handed it to her.

JESUS HEALS - JESUS SAVES
MIRACLES CAN HAPPEN TODAY - - MEETINGS NIGHTLY
CRUSADE WEEK BEGINNING MARCH 6th
7.30pm

She looked up at his anxious desperate face, tears filling her eyes. 'Oh, Tommy, I don't know. I will have to think about it, love. We never had much time for God, your dad and I, and when he died, well, I called God some awful names and blamed him for what happened. I don't think God is going to be much bothered with me now, anyway,' her voice faded away. How could she tell him there was no miracle cure for her, that she was wasting away, slowly but surely, dying. 'Anyway, I'll think about it.' She ruffled his hair and put her arms gingerly around him in the best way she could manage for a hug.

She had told Tommy about his dad's accident. A bit at a time, he had gradually put the whole story together. He knew she had never really got over it. For months afterwards, when he was little, she had shut herself away from everyone refusing all offers of help or sympathy. Whenever she talked about that night, tears of anger and frustration would choke her words. His dad had been a big chap, strong and yet gentle. Generous too, although goodness knows they never had much for themselves.

He had stopped his lorry on the motorway. A long-distance lorry driver, he had been. There had been an accident, a big pile up in the bad weather. It had been snowing and the roads were icy. He got down from his cab to help, trying to free people from their cars before a fire started. Then a car, not heeding the warning signs and in a great hurry, came down the outside lane and smashed into the group killing Tommy's dad and injuring others as they tried to help. A tragic accident and something which had taken her a long time to get over, although you never really do 'get over' something like that do you? Questions like, how and why could something like that have happened, and 'if only' constantly playing like an old broken record round and round in her mind.

'Mum, you have got to come, even if it doesn't work, you have got to try everything, you mustn't, mustn't ...' He couldn't say that awful word. He had thought about the possibility so many times as he lay on his bed at night. Although she had never allowed him to ask her properly, he knew.

He had heard her at night, groaning and walking around her room when she couldn't sleep. He had seen her eyes wet with crying some evenings when he came home from school. Sometimes there was no tea ready and, increasingly recently, nothing in the house to cook. She couldn't manage the shopping or carry heavy bags, and the thought of cooking sometimes made her nauseated and sent her rushing off to the bathroom. He had tried to tell her there were people who could help but she always shook her head. 'Not yet, I don't want anyone interfering, we can manage, son. I don't want anyone taking us away from each other, not yet.'

'Can I go, Mum? Ben, the new boy at school, said he was going and that his dad would take me too, if you said, yes, that is.' He had been so certain she would say yes. At school with Ben, it had all seemed so easy and uncomplicated. Making their plan had given them both a sense of purpose, breaking the monotony of a maths lesson which otherwise would have seemed endless. Now as the familiar frown which had furrowed deep lines across her forehead appeared, he hesitated, his confidence evaporating into thin air.

'Well, I don't know Tommy, I haven't met this gentleman, I don't know him from Adam. You have to be careful these days you know.'
'It will be alright Mum, really it will. I'll ask him to come in and meet you when he collects me, and I know it'll help Ben too. The boys at school don't let you into the gang very quickly when you're new and they rib him something awful about his going to church and that. He seemed sort of pleased when I said I wanted to come - like he couldn't quite believe it. Oh, please Mum, please ...'
'Well, if it means that much to you, then yes, of course you can go, and I shall expect a full report when you get home. This time, make sure you wake me even if I am asleep.'
'Gee, thanks Mum, thanks.'
'All this excitement has worn me out. Can you make us both a nice cup of tea now? You had better get some chips for your tea, there's some money in the jar on the shelf there.'
'It's ok I am not very hungry at the moment. I'll go down later. I'll get that tea now, and thanks Mum, I - I do love you.' He finished rather quietly as he went out to the kitchen, wondering whether boys usually said that kind of thing to their mother but sensing rather than knowing that some things need to be said sometimes even when you are not too sure about it. His mother lent her head on the back of the chair, closing her eyes. He's a good kid she thought, funny I don't ever remember someone getting as excited as all that about going to a church meeting. Still Tommy didn't get out much and at least it would be a break for him. Tears welled up, pushing their way out from under her eyelids and sliding gently down her sunken cheeks. It all seemed so unfair, why should Tommy who

never really knew his father have to go through this with her as well. Where would he go? Who would give him the love he needed, every child had the right to their own mum and dad. Children's Homes did a good job, most of the time, but it wasn't the same - she knew that. She would have to go into hospital soon. She couldn't manage on her own much longer.

'Oh, Dear God, if you are there, I just want to say sorry for all the rotten things I have said and thought about you, blaming you and all that, and if you are there, please help us now, me and Tommy ...'

When Tommy returned with a steaming mug of hot tea, she had dropped into a peaceful doze. He put the mug down beside her and pulled a blanket up over her legs and body, he was pleased she was getting some rest at last. He slipped quietly out of the room and went upstairs to his own room. He sat on the edge of his bed and looked down below on the small squares of garden, their own overgrown patch stood out in contrast to the neat tidy beds of flowers and cut grass along each side. His eyes wandered down the lane beyond, most of the other kids his age were out on their bikes or kicking a football around. He lay on his bed, his hands clasped under his head and drifted into his favourite world. He imagined a warm cosy room, the television on, people laughing and talking to each other, a table laid and then a beautiful, happy woman coming into the room carrying a tray of dishes, steam oozing out from under the lids, the smell of steak and kidney pie filling the room.

***

Chapter 2

Tommy couldn't wait for Monday evening to come. Ben was pleased to have someone to go with and his dad, as promised, stopped to meet Tommy's mother and assured her that he would keep a good eye on him and bring him home at the end of their evening, soon after nine o'clock. As the three of them set off down the road together he asked casually, 'Are you boys hungry? How about a hamburger on the way, keep the wolf from the door until we get back later, eh?'

'Oh yes, yes please,' came the reply in chorus, 'thanks a lot Mr er ...', said a delighted Tommy as he loosened the paper around his hot, soft, squidgy bun.

'Better call me Ralph,' Ben's father replied warming to this polite, quiet friend his son had made at school. He noticed the deep sadness which seemed to settle on him between sudden bursts of excitement or pleasure.

'Things a bit tough at home are they, Tommy? Your mum didn't look too good, alright, is she?'

Tommy, about to take his second-to-last mouthful of hamburger and enjoying every crumb, stopped and looked up, open mouthed, no one had ever asked him so directly, so simply before. There was a moments awkward silence while Tommy swallowed hard and thought about keeping their secret a bit longer but then clearing his throat, he began hesitantly at first to pour out the whole story. 'I showed her the leaflet about the meetings, she said she would think about it, she has got to come however bad she feels,' he finished simply.

He felt as if a tremendous burden had been lifted off his young, overloaded shoulders. Ralph didn't speak for a moment or two, he had known things weren't quite right from comments Ben had dropped out, but he could never have imagined what this young boy was coping with. He knew he needed support and some real practical help, but he framed his answer carefully so as not to patronise Tommy or cause him to regret his openness to a comparative stranger.

'You can tell your mum that I will come and collect you both any night she feels ready to come. Just let Ben know or give us a ring an hour or so before and I will be round. I will make sure she has a comfortable seat near the door and arrange for someone to sit with her in case she feels it is all too much to cope with. Then we will have another chat and see if we can't find one or two things which would make your job as man around the house a bit easier, eh?'

'Gee, thanks,' came the enthusiastic reply, 'I'll sure tell her.' Ralph looked across at Ben and winked a 'well done,' to his son who had listened to every word of Tommy's story without comment or interruption. They walked on a thoughtful silence growing between them.

Tommy began to notice other people walking along, heading in the same direction. Just up ahead he could hear music and singing. It sounded lively and happy, he picked out drums, guitars and a keyboard with a steady rhythmic beat. He wondered where it was coming from. They rounded the corner and there on the edge of the playing field was a large brightly lit marquee. Tommy had never seen, let alone been inside, such a huge kind of tent. People were milling around everywhere, smiling and talking, greeting each other and finding their way inside to the seats neatly arranged in many semi-circular rows. Up higher on the brightly lit platform, Tommy saw the source of the music he had been enjoying moments earlier. His eyes were like saucers. This was not like any church he had ever been in. It was noisy and happy, there were people everywhere. Large colourful banners hung either side of a platform which was decorated with tubs of yellow, orange and white flowers. He sat down, looking, listening, trying to take everything in, trying to absorb this whole new world. He felt happy for the first time in months, he sighed and waited. A strange feeling of excitement began to well up on the inside of him and his heart beat a little faster.

At home, his mum Sarah had relaxed as Tommy left the house, she knew he was in good company and well occupied for the evening. She had woken up from her doze in the armchair and despite Tommy having covered her with a blanket she felt cold and decided to make her way upstairs to her so familiar bed. As she lay back against the many pillows, she fell into a fitful sleep the constant worry which invaded her mind was that, without family around him and with little opportunity of bringing his friends home, he would go out one night and get mixed up in trouble. Sometimes she had nightmares. She would see him in some detention centre, sitting alone on a hard bed in a sparse dormitory. She would cry and cry sometimes thinking of him left to manage by himself. Later, lying awake, she wondered what the homes were like. Perhaps she should make arrangements for Tommy to visit and begin to get to know the staff. If only they knew someone who would at least visit him once the move to a children's home became inevitable. She made a mental note to do something about that, to find out where Tommy would have to go. Her thoughts were interrupted by a loud gurgling noise making its way up from the region of her stomach, reminding her that she had eaten very little that day and that she still needed some sustenance sometimes. She suddenly had an overwhelming longing for a piece of hot toast and marmalade and a cup of tea. She smiled to herself, despite everything, she wasn't dead yet.

She swung her legs over the side of the bed, wrapped the faded dressing gown around her, slid her feet into slippers and made her way cautiously to the top of the stairs. She dreaded these stairs. Once she had taken them two at a time, bounding up them to see to Tommy when he had been crying or sick, racing down when the telephone had rung, and she was expecting Jack to let her know he was within hours of being back home. She had been agile and fit, full of life, proud of her home and family.

Now she stood at the top. Her head began to spin, she felt dizzy, she turned to grasp the rail with both hands, she went down sideways now, steadying and supporting herself as she trod one stair at a time. The cord of her dressing gown, fastened clumsily and loosely about her waist hung down draping itself around her feet. As she moved her left foot down it became entangled in the dangling loop. She was already leaning, her foot searching for the stair beneath her, instead, with a gasp and cry she catapulted sideways, sliding and rolling her way down to the bottom. She lay still, her breathing was shallow and rasping, her skin grey and cold as she slipped into unconsciousness.

***

Chapter 3

A few miles away, in the warm, peaceful atmosphere of the tent there hung an air of anticipation. Tommy's whole attention had been caught by the man standing now and speaking from the platform. At first, he had been quite amused by the short, plump, balding man who had stood up to speak. He couldn't imagine anyone looking less like a preacher than this man. He had cracked a few jokes at the beginning, making everyone laugh and feel at ease. He had told them they could dance during the singing, stand or sit as they wanted, lift up their hands if they felt like it and have their eyes open or shut it didn't matter one jot as far as God was concerned. He said that God wanted people to be right on the inside, he wanted them to sing to him and praise him from their hearts.

Now he was speaking much more seriously. Tommy forgot about the people around him, he forgot how amused he had been by this little man, he was listening intently. Every word this man spoke seemed to speak directly to Tommy. He felt sure someone had told him all his thoughts and fears. Someone must have heard him whispering in his bedroom at night, pouring out his loneliness and longing to be like the other boys with a dad and a mum. This man seemed to know exactly how Tommy felt. He spoke ordinarily. He didn't use difficult words or speak in a funny voice. Tommy sat on the edge of his seat, hungry for every word that was being spoken. The man explained that God knew all about him. That he had known him since he was just a tiny cell, hardly any size at all, and that He loved him and wanted to be his friend. He said God was his father and because he loved him so much, he had actually sent his own son Jesus to tell everyone what he was like and to make it possible for all who wanted to, to be adopted into his family. He said God and Jesus could be as real as any human father and friend. He explained that the barrier which existed between each person and God had been removed by Jesus. Like a wall which had separated him and us and had kept God hidden had been demolished. He said that everyone who wanted to, could step over the rubble and run right into God's outstretched arms. The thought of it, the possibility almost overwhelmed Tommy. He bowed his head wishing he knew the right thing to say. How should he address God?

Suddenly, it seemed he knew, an idea almost like a picture flashed into his mind. It was so clear and obvious - someone might have been standing right next to him whispering the answer in his ear. If God was willing to be a dad to him, he would talk to him just as he would have done to his own dad. Tommy raised his head - that was a bit of a puzzle too, he wondered what his dad would have been like. Would he have been very strict and distant, or would he and his dad have been good mates? Would he have had to wait for the right moment to speak or would he have been able to rush up to him and ask about anything, anytime. Tommy scratched his head thoughtfully. Then he decided that he would imagine that his dad was a bit like Ralph - he liked Ralph and already he had been able to tell him things no one else knew and he felt he could trust him too.

He lowered his head and told God that he wasn't exactly sure what it was like to have a dad, but that if he had one, he knew that he would want so much for his mum to get better and be his mum again. He knew there was a lot he still didn't fully understand but there were several more nights to go and if he came again tomorrow - and the next night - he couldn't wait and he hoped Ralph wouldn't mind bringing him every night. He shot a quick glance in Ralph's direction. Ralph smiled back. He saw Tommy's glowing face, his whole expression full of renewed hope. As the meeting drew to a close, he lent towards Tommy,

'Do you think you will want to come again, then Tommy?'

'You bet, I mean yes, please I'd love to - tomorrow night perhaps?
Ralph nodded and put his arm around Tommy's shoulders.
'I think we can manage that, eh Ben. I had better get you two boys home now otherwise you'll be in no fit state for school tomorrow.'

They joined the slowly moving stream of people making for the exit. Tommy glanced back, reluctant to leave, savouring the atmosphere which had filled the tent. All round people stood in small groups talking or with bowed heads still praying together. He had never experienced anything quite like this. He determined no matter what, his mum would come, just once, he knew whatever happened it would do her good.

***

Chapter 4

The two boys walked ahead together, their heads close and conspiratorial. Tommy threw one question after another at Ben. Holding up his hands in mock horror, Ben gasped.
'Hang on a minute, let me answer those one at a time as far as I can. I don't know the answers to all your questions, but I'll tell you all I know.' As they turned the corner into the next street the car came into view.
'Race you to the car,' Ben challenged, laughing and panting - the two boys landed in a heap on the bonnet of the car. As their laughter subsided, Ben continued cautiously,
'I am really glad you asked all those questions and that I - well, none of my friends have ever taken it all that seriously before, in fact I got teased quite a lot, called a religious nut and loony and things like that, but I'm not, I know that. If only any of them had really listened,

instead of just pretending and making fun of me. You're not just pretending are you, Tommy?'

'Me pretending, no way, this has been the best evening I've spent in ages, all that back there was for real, I just know that. It has got to be real Ben, it is the only way I have to help my mum. She … '

Ralph walked up to the boys, pleased to see them getting on so well together. He opened the car door. They slid quietly side by side into the back seat, both full of their own thoughts and feelings. Each sensing the possibility that they had found in the other a real friend. There were so many things waiting to be shared, waiting to be discovered.

They turned down Maple Road and pulled up outside Tommy's house. There were no lights shining out from the front room or the hall which caused Tommy a momentary frown. His mum must have dropped off to sleep while it was still light and not woken up to turn them on ready for when he got back. Tommy turned as he got out of the car.

'Thanks for a great evening,' he smiled at Ralph and gave Ben a cheery wave.

'Same time tomorrow, we will pick you up again, give our regards to your mother.' Ralph kept the engine running and waited while Tommy went up the steps to his front door, watching while the key slid into the lock and turned, then he let in the clutch and pulled away.

Tommy pushed the heavy door open. His hand moved up and down the inside wall trying to locate the light switch. He knew it was on the left-hand side, about level with his shoulder. Why on earth hadn't his mother left just one light on. He began to feel a twinge of annoyance and disappointment. She couldn't have forgotten he was still out, he had been looking forward so much to telling her all about the evening. His hand brushed past the switch, he moved back slightly and with an almost imperceptible move of his finger flooded the dark shadowy hall with light.

A glace towards the stairs told him everything. A cry of horror and dismay left his open mouth. In one brief moment his happiness became despair. He couldn't believe what he saw. How long had she been lying like that, was she still alive?
'Oh Mum, Mum, it's me Tommy, I am home, don't die Mum, please don't die - I'll get help. He moved quickly towards her, falling down on his knees beside her, his overwhelming fear was that he was too late. That she was already dead. He put his hand and then his cheek in front of her mouth and nose as he had seen people do in films. A faint breeze cooled his burning cheeks. She was alive … just. He grabbed the blanket still lying over the armchair and covered her gently - she was so cold. He tried to straighten her twisted body, gently, carefully aware that he could do her more harm than good. He just couldn't bear to see her lying like that. He put a cushion under her head, that would make her more comfortable, he talked to her, despite the shock, his concern for her kept him going.

As he drove away, Ralph whistled to himself. 'A good evening that, wouldn't you agree, son?' 'Yes, Dad, it was great, I think Tommy really enjoyed being with us and in the meeting, but it was funny there were no lights on for Tommy when he got back, do you think everything is alright?' At the end of the road Ralph slowed the car. 'I'm not sure Ben, I agree, perhaps I pulled away a bit too fast and we should have gone in with him, but I didn't want to crowd him. I reckon we will go back and make sure everything is ok.'
'Snap, I think we should too, Dad, I feel really odd inside, sort of worried without knowing why.'

'Right, that's it then. If we both feel that same way, back we go, we had better hurry.' He turned the car around and raced back down the empty road, the breaks screeched as they pulled up outside Tommy's house. Now the light shone from out from above the front door. As Ralph got out of the car his feeling of concern increased. He crossed the pavement to the steps with Ben close behind him. Suddenly the front door was flung open. Standing outlined by the light from inside, Tommy looked very small and frightened.

'It's alright Tommy, what's happened, we are here to help.' Ralph took the steps two at a time. He gripped Tommy by the shoulders, trying to reassure him and hold him together. As Tommy turned to show him where his mother was lying, Ralph saw her.

'Oh no, Tommy, where is the phone?' Tommy pointed to the living room. His throat dry, no sound came out. The shock, and now relief, began to affect his body causing him to shiver violently. He couldn't believe that Ralph was back here now and was taking charge. Tommy recalled how, when he had finished making his mum as comfortable as he knew how, panic had taken hold of him, wondering what to do and who could he get to help? Butterflies had filled his stomach. He had made for the front door believing someone must be passing by … and there, there had been Ralph. Ralph who minutes earlier had driven away with a cheery wave. His body gave another violent shiver.
'An ambulance is on its way, it won't be too long getting here. There is only one thing I know for us to do right now. Tommy, you have done well trying to cover her and make her more comfortable, just hold her hand and see if you can warm her a bit, Ben and I will pray …' He slipped his thick jacket off placing it around the shoulders of the trembling boy. He moved towards Sarah's still body taking

Tommy with him. He knew that later it would do Tommy good to remember that he had been able to help and comfort his mum.

The ambulance men were very kind, lifting Sarah gently and skilfully. They asked Tommy questions. How long had she been ill? Who was her doctor? How long had she been lying at the bottom of the stairs? Together Ralph helped Tommy answer the questions to the best of their ability and as the ambulance men were tending to Sarah, Ralph phoned his home. He explained that something had happened, he would fill his wife in with all the details later –
'And Diane, one more thing, could you move the spare mattress into Ben's room and make up a bed for our young friend here, I think he is going to need a place to stay for the next few days. Thanks, love, got to go now, we will see you later.'

Ralph followed the ambulance as it moved quickly through the familiar streets. At the hospital the trauma team, having already been alerted were standing by, ready for Sarah's arrival. The ambulance drove with lights flashing and siren sounding right up to the accident and emergency entrance. Sarah was lifted carefully onto a trolley and taken quickly into the resuscitation area for examination and emergency treatment. Ralph helped Tommy give their details to the receptionist. Tommy felt numb and cold. A young nurse took all three of them into a relative's room. She brought them drinks of tea in paper cups, and then sat down with them to unravel the history of this desperately poorly lady.

Tommy told the nurse about the pains and the vomiting. How she had gone to the doctor quite a long time ago. Tommy had known she had been crying but she just said it was nothing and he wasn't to worry himself about her. Since then, he had seen her getting thinner and more weary. He said she didn't eat much anymore and often stayed in bed most of the day. He yawned and rested his head on his arm as a wave of weariness suddenly engulfed him. Ralph continued with Tommy's story as far as he knew it.

'He can come home with us tonight, and for as long as necessary until things get sorted out,' he finished.

Tommy was taken to his mother's cubicle and was told that she would be moved up to a ward later, she was being monitored by different machines and had some fluid going in through a needle in her arm. She looked much more comfortable although still pale and unconscious. He kissed her on the cheek.

'I'll be back tomorrow, Mum, please get better. I love you.' His voice, just a whisper, brought a lump to Ralph's throat as he spoke to the nurse.

'We will ring up in the morning to see whether there has been any change. Thanks for looking after us so well.' The young nurse blushed and smiled as she showed the way out to the main door. As they passed the doctors' station, a young doctor was talking on the phone.

'Yes, stage four cancer, untreated as far as I can see from any notes ...'

They moved out of ear shot. Ralph knew he could have been talking about anybody but somehow, he felt the conversation concerned Tommy's mum and he wondered what the next few days would bring.

Ben's mum gave everyone, including Tommy, a quick hug as they came through the door. She held Tommy at arm's length and looked at him with a discerning eye. This has been quite a day for you, hasn't it, Tommy? Don't you worry we will be around with you until things get themselves sorted out, ok? Tommy nodded unable to speak with fear and relief all swirling around in his exhausted mind. She had hot soup, bread and cheese waiting for them and laid out on the kitchen table. Usually, Tommy's favourite but he couldn't manage much of anything tonight. He borrowed some of Ben's pyjamas and slid gratefully into the warm sleeping bag which had been laid out ready for him.

'Thank you so much for … everything, I don't know what I would have done … seeing you and Ben coming when I opened the door … I thought you had gone …' his voice broke, tears springing with utter relief into his eyes.

'I know son, I know, we just had a feeling that things weren't quite right. So, we turned around and came back to you. Your mum is in good hands now though. You try and get some sleep. Ben will be up too in a minute, sleep till you wake in the morning. I'll give school a ring and let them know you won't be coming in.'

Back downstairs Ralph and Ben told Diane the whole story filling in the gaps for each other.

***

Chapter 5

Tommy was adamant that he wanted to go to the tent meeting again that night. He knew it was the one place he had found some hope. His deep, deep sadness was that now it was going to be impossible for his mum to come with him. He had seen her earlier in the day, she looked as if she was having a long peaceful sleep. The doctor had told Tommy that there was a very strong possibility that she might not wake up, that she was so ill it could be the best for her. He said that she wasn't in any pain and that was a good thing, wasn't it? Tommy had nodded not trusting himself to speak. Ralph said that they could pop back after the meeting tonight to see if there had been any change and to say goodnight to her. They were allowed free visiting while the situation remained so critical.

Tommy was pleased to be back inside the tent, although he found it much harder to concentrate this time. His mind kept wandering back to the room in the hospital and the picture of his mum, at the bottom of the stairs, was there every time he closed his eyes.

After the singing and the music, a different man stood up to speak. Older and more traditionally dressed Tommy felt disappointed, wondering if tonight was going to be a big let-down after all. He had begun to trust what he was hearing but perhaps tonight would be difficult to listen to and understand. Tommy slid down in his seat, what could he think about to keep those awful pictures out of his mind. He began daydreaming his escape dream, closing his eyes he saw a picture of his mother as she was in his favourite photograph, alive and well. At the back of his mind Tommy realised the man had started to speak now. The question arose in his mind, should he shut that voice out straight away or allow himself to hear a few words which would confirm his worst fears. Nothing could ever mean as much to him as last night had - on the other hand it had been so good and he had so much to learn, maybe it was going to be even more important to him now - and Ben, Ben had been so happy to explain things he didn't understand and so pleased to see that he was interested. He pulled himself back from his dream and sat up in his seat, of course he wanted to hear what the man had to say - that was why he had come wasn't it?

Please turn with me in your Bibles to ... Tonight I want to show you that Jesus not only went about healing the sick but taught and encouraged his disciples to do so as well. I want to show you that both the disciples and then also the Christians in the early church prayed for sick people to be healed. Jesus commanded his disciples to continue the work He had begun. If we today consider ourselves to be his disciples, and if it is true that Jesus is the same yesterday, today and forever, then we can expect God to be able and ready to work in the same way now. That is some good news, isn't it? Tonight, we are going to pray for the sick here and we know we are going to see some wonderful things take place this evening.

As he spoke, he showed them how many times Jesus healed the people who came to him. How different the situations and needs of the people were and how each one was touched and spoken to in a unique way. The man told them of his own experience and of the miracles he had witnessed.
'Nothing is impossible for God,' he concluded, 'sometimes God works through our faith, sometimes through that of the sick person themselves, and sometimes through the faith of others closely involved with them.

Tommy felt his heart lift again ... might it still not be too late to see his mum get better? Inside his head, though, a voice kept telling him not to be so silly - he had seen how ill she was and remembered so clearly the doctor's words, that she might not wake up from this sleep and he knew she would never make it to the tent now anyway. As people began to leave their seats and move forward to be prayed for, Tommy bowed his head and closed his eyes.

'Dear God, thank you for showing me how to pray, for telling me what to say to you last night. How shall I do it tonight, about Mum? I think, I believe you can make her better, but I am still not sure that you will. We aren't very important or clever and maybe you have never really noticed us before. I can't think why you should bother with us, there are loads and loads of ill people in hospital. But then they aren't all my mum. I don't want her to die, so please if you are listening, and you really can do it, help her right now and make her well again. Thank you.'

For the second time that week he felt as if a burden had been lifted off his shoulders. As he finished his own prayer, he became aware of others around him. Ralph and Ben were next to him, the man who had spoken the night before was on one side and several people he didn't know were standing with him praying quietly, supporting Tommy and standing with him. Overwhelmed by their love and concern, he lowered his head again, wiping his sleeve quickly across his eyes, wondering how long they had been standing there and when they were going to stop. Despite his embarrassment, he was pleased too. Pleased that it didn't all hang on his prayers. God must have heard now, mustn't he? As they left those around him patted him on the back and smiled encouragingly at him, as if they already knew his story.

It was quieter than usual in the Accident and Emergency department, the staff were free to tidy and re-stock the cubicles for a while. The three late night visitors followed the signs to the female medical ward where Sarah now lay in a side room. As they turned down the second corridor on the left, they heard laughter and excited conversation. 'Strange?' they thought, looking at one another with some puzzlement. It seemed inappropriate both for this time of the evening and with the knowledge of the seriously ill patients in the single rooms along this corridor. The door of Sarah's room was open. The light shone out bright and welcoming.

'Do you think they have moved her to another room or has she …'
Tommy's voice, full of anxiety, broke the silence and echoed all their
thoughts out loud.

'I am not too sure,' Ralph responded quickly, 'I am sure they will
soon update us.'

'Is Mrs Gould still in Room 7?' Ralph asked the smiling nurse as she
passed them along the corridor. 'Oh yes, she is, sir. Are you the
gentleman who brought her in? Staff Nurse would like a word with
you please. She is in her office, second door along on the left, once
you have been in to see Mrs Gould could you go and knock on her
door. The boys too, if you don't mind.'

Tommy slipped his hand into Ralph's as they drew level with the
door of Sarah's room. His heart began to beat so loudly he thought
everyone must be able to hear it. They stood quite still looking
towards the bed. Tommy gasped, not able to believe what he was
seeing. He let go of Ralph's hand and launched himself across the
room. 'Mum, Mum, you're better, you're better, it worked, He did
hear us and answer our prayer.'

'Come, Ben, you and I will make ourselves scarce for a moment or
two', Ralph said. 'Let's go and see what the staff nurse has to tell us
… that we don't know already that is!' He added with a slightly
triumphant note in his voice.

'Oh Mum, so much has happened, there is so much to tell you, do
you really feel better, not just a little bit but properly I mean, you do
look pink again, still a bit fragile but not so ill anymore.'

'Come here now young man, and I will show you how much better I
am!' She held her arms out wide and wrapped them around him as
he buried his head in her chest, no longer fearing that he would
break something or cause her pain. Holding him close as if she would

never let him go again. She added, 'I am sooo hungry, I am sure I could manage a real big, juicy steak and kidney pie, homemade of course!'

Tommy laughed, I don't think we can get that tonight, Mum, but we can sure get you something to eat at last.' As he finished speaking and laughing all at the same time, he remembered his favourite escape dream of sitting in his own home with his Mum, and maybe now with their newfound friends, eating their hot steaming pies and sharing life together. 'In fact,' his Mum's voice broke through his thoughts, 'I might even manage to get to that meeting of yours tomorrow evening, if your new friends can still take us both.'

Tommy took a moment to look up and offer an overwhelmingly grateful, 'Thank you God, you are something truly amazing.'

***

Epilogue - Tommy

Although we don't know the outcome for Tommy and his Mum, we do know that her condition was greatly improved and that, whatever happens in the future, Tommy now has friends who will make sure that he is well looked after.

When we pray for healing, we see some people healed and others not so. This is a mystery only God will one day tell us the answer to.

I recently had the privilege of praying with a neighbour who had been told by doctors that there was nothing else they could offer him in the way of treatment. We talked about his eternal position as well as the physical one and that, just like Nicodemus in John's Gospel Chapter 3:1-17 (RSV), he needed to be born again spiritually. As a young boy my neighbour had gone to Sunday School and Boys' Brigade and so understood who Jesus is but wasn't too sure what it meant to believe in Him.

In John's Gospel Chapter 3:16 it tells us, 'For God so loved the world that He gave His only Son, that whoever believes in Him should not perish but have everlasting life.' We can each put our names in the place where it says 'the world' because this is what Jesus did for each one of us - for you and for me.

If we think we have lived a 'good' life, we might not understand why we needed someone to die for our sin. Yet, if we are honest, however well we have lived, we know that we have had bad moments, thoughts, attitudes and sometimes actions as well. None of us can say we have *never* done anything wrong. More than this, God says that living our lives without acknowledging Him and who

He is, is what separates us from Him and is the greatest sin of all. He explains it better than I can in the rest of that 3rd Chapter of John's Gospel.

If, like my neighbour, you are not sure where you stand in your belief or unbelief you can pray this prayer:

"Dear Father God, thank you so much for sending your Son into this world to lead me back to you. Thank you, that if I had been the only one alive on this planet, He would still have needed to die so that my sin could be forgiven, and I could have a relationship again with you. Jesus, thank you that you gave up your life for me. Please come into my life and take it over from now on."

If you have prayed that prayer or if you want to understand more about 'believing in Jesus' or 'being born again', please contact a Christian friend or log into renewalcc.com/nextsteps. Alternatively, find an Alpha Course near you where you will receive a warm welcome and the opportunity to explore the many questions around faith.

***

Hot Coffee

Sighing deeply with momentary relief, Beth drew into herself the solitude and the quiet all around her. Pouring the hot coffee into the mug she savoured the delicious aroma. The sight and smell of the beans, ground and roasted, always brought her a flood of memories. Memories of her childhood spent on a large coffee plantation in Kenya. Happy days of colour and sun, freedom and fun. People coming and going, visits to the town and sometimes into the bush to visit a sick worker. Other memories began to push their way up from her subconscious mind, but she spoke sharply to herself, 'Not tonight, no.' Tonight was her night, and she was going to make the most of it.

Dominique, her difficult and demanding eighteen-month-old son, was finally asleep and as Gerald was working late, the evening was all hers. Clasping the hot mug, she warmed and comforted herself, moving her shoulders up and down to help ease the tension tightening the muscles in her neck and back. Gerald would sometimes massage her neck and shoulders telling her she worried too much.
'You should relax more,' he would say. 'It is just the terrible twos starting a bit early.' Others would murmur, smiling knowingly at her, offering sympathy but no suggestions on surviving it. She supposed that one day things would just get better. They had been so happy, before they moved here, she had reeled in the compliments as the mother of such a model baby ... as if it were she who made him sleep and gurgle at all the right times! What, she wondered, had

happened to change it all. Now he cried a lot, often waking in the night as if he was having a horrible nightmare.

She took one hand off the mug and reached out to pick up the paper to catch up on the local news. She moved towards the kitchen door flicking off the light switch as she passed it. The next moment a piercing cry echoed through the quiet house, catching her off guard this time. She jerked violently, gasping as the hot coffee splashed over her hand.

'Not tonight, oh, please dear God, not tonight.' There had been many disturbed evenings in this house. She wondered to herself, how could such little ones have nightmares when they didn't have any life experiences to break through into their subconscious minds so powerfully. She just wasn't sure anymore how to react, or if she could cope. She deposited her mug on the hall table and took the stairs two at a time.

'It's alright, darling, Mummy's coming.' Reaching the landing, she shivered as a draught of cold air took her by surprise, she couldn't remember having left any windows open this late. She grasped the knob of Dominique's bedroom door and turned it. As she did so, her free arm was already stretched out to locate the switch and turn on the light. As the door opened the lights flickered and then went out plunging the house into almost total darkness.

'It must be a fuse. Hold on there, Dom, I will get a torch and be right back here with you.' She turned to leave the room, the same cold blast she had felt moments earlier curled itself around her legs and then up around her body as powerful forces propelled her back into the room. She fell against the side of the cot and, even as she cried out struggling to maintain her balance, she was already reaching down to him, scooping him up in her arms, determined that whatever was going on here, he would be close to her. He was warm and soft against her, although whimpering and moaning as if in some kind of pain or discomfort.

'It's alright Dom, Mummy's here, it's alright, darling.' Even as she spoke, she felt as if her arms were being pulled from around him - as if something or someone was trying to make her release him.
'No, no, leave us alone,' she heard herself whisper hoarsely, her voice strangled by the fear that was rising up on the inside of her. A fierce oppression pushed in on her from all sides, threatening to crush the life out of her.

A watery moon brought a little light into the cold room and as Beth's eyes became used to the darkness, she thought she could make out ghostly shapes skulking in the corners, watching her with malevolent, cunning expressions. It was difficult to see how many there were, they seemed to merge into each other and yet be capable of moving away from the group and be as individuals too. She shuddered, closing her eyes in an attempt to blot out the picture coming into her mind ...

The rhythmic sound of the tribal drums began to beat in her head. She saw herself curled up on the floor of a mud hut, pulling a blanket up around her ears and then covering them with her hands, trying desperately to blot out the incessant beating as the rhythm and volume worked towards a crescendo. She remembered how her father had been invited to a special ceremony in one of the out-lying villages.
'Come with me, Beth,' he had said, 'I'd be glad of your company, we can make it into a mini holiday together.' On their way back from

that visit they had been delayed by heavy rains, unable to cross the river in the usual place and had been forced to take shelter with their African guide in a smaller, more remote village at the foot of Mount Kenya. It was a memory which had long been buried in the recesses of Beth's mind. The sight of the shadowy figures dancing to the point of frenzy around a stone slab, their bare feet pounding the soft earth had sent vibrations across the compound, their writhing silhouettes had drawn close in a gradually tightening circle around the altar of their ritual.

She remembered now that same piercing cry which had cut through the night air as the drums reached their highest point of tension and had suddenly stopped. She thought she had blotted out forever the pitiful moaning which had followed that terrible sound.

Her father had packed hurriedly the following morning and, safe or not, they continued their journey. He had refused to answer her questions. Tight-lipped and obviously considerably shaken himself, he had told her that some things were not for discussion with young ladies and that she was never to mention anything of what she may have thought she had seen or heard to anyone at all …

Now, in Dominique's bedroom, her skin crawled and the weight of the oppression began to suffocate her as she knew where she had seen those ghostly forms before. They had been there, hovering above and around those dancing figures, they had been swooping, separating and then merging again as they had covered and surrounded the stone slab. She felt the same stifling fear, the same terrifying power, that she had felt as she had lain listening and peeping through the doorway of the African hut. As she sank to her knees her mind struggled to regain control. This, this is England, these - these things don't happen here.

'What do you want?' her own strangled voice, questioned the darkness. A sighing hiss echoed round the room. She shuddered, tightening her hold on Dominique, wanting now to be comforted by his tiny body. But with a gasp she realised her arms now were empty and wrapped only around her own body. Instinctively, she managed to cover her ears just as she had those many years ago and, as then, it did nothing to quieten the pounding repetitive beat. The cold draught around her had become an icy blast, she was shaking uncontrollably now, sharp pains cutting through her body as if icicles were being pushed into her flesh. She heard herself moaning in the plaintive way she had heard Dominique moments earlier. Dominique, where was he, why wasn't he here in her arms?

Peering through the eerie light she scanned the room. Her attention was caught by a flurry of activity in the far corner of the room. Weaving and dancing the ghosts came and went as if there was no ceiling and no walls around them. On the changing table below them was Dominique, his legs and arms spread wide, he lay motionless and unprotesting as if in a trance of some sort. Her hands flew to cover her mouth as her anguished cry spilled into the midst of the unchallenged proceedings. Suddenly she knew what she had never been told. As the knife had been raised over that living sacrifice in a remote African village, her father had risked his life snatching the Infant from the altar and had prevented the gruesome ceremony achieving its ultimate goal. Now the spirits had come for revenge. The sound of her own voice encouraged her, an almost imperceptible shudder went around the room.

Downstairs she thought she heard the front door opening, she waited, wondering what else could happen. Expecting the worst and feeling powerless to stop it. The door slammed.

'Beth what's happened to these damn lights, where are you? I finished earlier than I thought I would. Where's the torch gone?' His voice sounded the most wonderful thing Beth thought she had ever heard. A cold hand clamped her mouth, she looked across the room, the dancing had stopped but there was no mistaking the raised arm as if awaiting an order before plunging down into that small motionless body.

'Jesus Christ, I didn't remember there was a table right by the cupboard …'

The hand dropped from Beth's face, the beings faltered and began to fall away from the table, whilst others began to move through the walls. Beth found that she had some freedom to move - almost to cry out. Something was happening here, she longed for Gerald to speak again, to shout or swear. The line of a school hymn sung week after week came hesitatingly, falteringly into her mind. How had it gone, that's it, *At the Name of Jesus every knee shall bow*. She hadn't understood it at all at the time but now, perhaps, it was making some sense. She whispered the name "Jesus, Jesus" then more boldly, loudly. The beings were shaken and more of them began to go. They crumpled before her eyes, whining and crying. Her body began to feel released, her voice grew stronger. A new feeling of peace began to still her pounding heart.

'We are up here in Dom's room,' she sobbed out loud as she could. Slowly, deliberately, she began to say the Lord's Prayer. The one she remembered her religious studies teacher saying was the prayer Jesus had taught his disciples when they had asked him to teach them how to pray. She started slowly, hesitatingly, but as she spoke the words came back to her.

'Our Father who art in Heaven, hallowed be thy Name,
Thy Kingdom come, thy will be done on earth, as it is in heaven.
Give us this day our daily bread and forgive us our trespasses as we forgive those who trespass against us.
Lead us not into temptation and deliver us from evil,' she shivered as she spoke out those words, knowing how much evil had just been in that small bedroom.
'For Thine is the kingdom, the power and the glory. For ever and ever, Amen.'

She remembered it in the old traditional version because now she remembered that they had often repeated it in school assemblies. Her eyes closed as she spoke it out. She didn't see that Gerald had come into the room. He stood now transfixed in the doorway waiting for her to finish.

'What in the world is going on here?' he gasped. She moved across the room and fell into his arms.
'Just hold me please, hold me tight.' As he did just that, he glanced around the room. Dominique, eyes wide open, lay quietly looking up at him. As their eyes met the little boy gurgled and smiled, holding out his arms asking to be picked up and included in the embrace. Beth drew back from the embrace and, breathing in deeply, she looked around the room.

'I am so glad that you came back when you did - there is a lot to tell you and I don't fully understand it all myself. For once, I am so glad that when you crashed into the hall table you spoke out the name of Jesus ... although perhaps, not for the best reason.' She gave him a rueful smile as she scooped Dominique up into her arms. 'That Name immediately changed what was going on here around us in this room. That is why I was saying the Lord's Prayer when you came in here ... really to make absolutely sure they had gone.'

'They?' Gerald queried, 'there was no one else here when I came into the room.'

'Ah, but there had been, I can assure you. Let's go downstairs and I will tell you the story right from the beginning. One which I think has now come full circle ... and is finished!'

***

Hot Coffee – Epilogue

In moments of crises and fear, danger, extreme pain or challenging situations, it seems almost instinctive for us as human beings to call on God in some form or another. Many of us call on the name of Jesus or Christ or God - even in an inappropriate way. I think that this demonstrates how, deep down in the heart of man, there is a need for someone bigger and divine, and who is in control of the world and our circumstances. Although Gerard uses the name of Jesus in his frustration, and without any real faith or belief, I have allowed it to be in there to demonstrate how powerful that name can be. In the Bible, it says that even the demons have to obey that name. An illustration of this can be found in Chapter 4 of the Book of Luke, where there is a powerful story of Jesus dealing with a man tormented by an evil spirit. In *Hot Coffee*, as Gerard utters the name of Jesus, Beth notices enough of a change in the atmosphere for her to start to use that name in an effective and powerful way.

Philippians 2:10 (The Passion Translation of the Bible) says:
"The authority of the name of Jesus causes every knee to bow in reverence! Everything and everyone will one day submit to this name - in the heavenly realm, in the earthly realm and in the demonic realm. And every tongue will proclaim in every language: *'Jesus Christ is Lord Yahweh'* bringing glory and honour to God, his Father."

The story of Jesus driving out an evil spirit from a man (Luke 4:31-36) also confirms to us how He has power over the spirit realm … and that the Name of Jesus truly has the final word!

***